Red and White Roses:
Unity

For Bryan and Shade, famous
photographers with *drastically*
different points of view,
working together could be a
disaster. But then they united
their considerable talents—and
found they'd ignited a passion
they couldn't ignore!

NORA ROBERTS

LANGUAGE OF LOVE

**Love has a language all its own, and for
centuries, flowers have symbolized
love's finest expression.
Discover the language of flowers
—and love—
in this romantic collection of 48 favorite
books by bestselling author Nora Roberts.**

NORA ROBERTS

Language of Love

One Summer

Silhouette Books

To Deb Horm, for the mutual memories

SILHOUETTE BOOKS
300 East 42nd St., New York, N.Y. 10017

ONE SUMMER © 1986 by Nora Roberts
First published as a Silhouette Special Edition

Language of Love edition published November 1991

ISBN: 0-373-51031-4

Chapter One

The room was dark. Pitch dark. But the man named Shade was used to the dark. Sometimes he preferred it. It wasn't always necessary to see with your eyes. His fingers were both clever and competent, his inner eye as keen as a knife blade.

There were times, even when he wasn't working, when he'd sit in a dark room and simply let images form in his mind. Shapes, textures, colors. Sometimes they came clearer when you shut your eyes and just let your thoughts flow. He courted darkness, shadows, just as relentlessly as he courted the light. It was all part of life, and life—its images—was his profession.

He didn't always see life as others did. At times it was harsher, colder than the naked eye could see—or wanted to. Other times it was softer, more lovely than the busy world imagined. Shade observed it, grouped the elements, manipulated time and shape, then recorded it his way. Always his way.

Now, with the room dark and the sound of recorded jazz coming quiet and disembodied from the corner, he worked with his hands and his mind. Care and timing. He used them both in every aspect of his work. Slowly, smoothly, he opened the capsule and transferred the undeveloped film onto the reel. When the light-tight lid was on the developing tank, he set the timer with his free hand, then pulled the chain that added the amber light to the room.

Shade enjoyed developing the negative and making the print as much as, sometimes more than he enjoyed taking the photograph. Darkroom work required precision and accuracy. He needed both in his life. Making the print allowed for creativity and experimentation. He needed those as well. What he saw, what he felt about what he saw, could be translated exactly or left as an enigma. Above all, he needed the satisfaction of creating something himself, alone. He always worked alone.

Now, as he went through each precise step of developing—temperature, chemicals, agitation, timing—the amber light cast his face into shadows. If Shade had been looking to create the image of photographer at work, he'd never have found a clearer statement than himself.

His eyes were dark, intense now as he added the stop bath to the tank. His hair was dark as well, too long for the convention he cared nothing about. It brushed over his ears, the back of his T-shirt and fell over his forehead nearly to his eyebrows. He never gave much thought to style. His was cool, almost cold, and rough around the edges.

His face was deeply tanned, lean and hard, with strong bones dominating. His mouth was taut as he concentrated. There were lines spreading out finely from his eyes, etched there by what he'd seen and what he'd felt about it. Some would say there'd already been too much of both.

The nose was out of alignment, a result of a professional hazard. Not everyone liked to have his picture taken. The Cambodian soldier had broken Shade's nose, but Shade had gotten a telling picture of the city's devastation, of the waste. He still considered it an even exchange.

In the amber light, his movements were brisk. He had a rangy, athletic body, the result of years in the field—often a foreign, unfriendly field—miles of legwork and missed meals.

Even now, years after his last staff assignment for *International View*, Shade remained lean and agile. His work wasn't as grueling as it had been in his early years in Lebanon, Laos, Central America, but his pattern hadn't changed. He worked long hours, sometimes waiting endlessly for just the right shot, sometimes using a roll of film within minutes. If his style and manner were aggressive, it could be said that they'd kept him alive and whole during the wars he'd recorded.

The awards he'd won, the fee he now commanded, remained secondary to the picture. If no one had paid him or recognized his work, Shade would still have been in the darkroom, developing his film. He was respected, successful and rich. Yet he had no assistant and continued to work out of the same darkroom he'd set up ten years before.

When Shade hung his negatives up to dry, he already had an idea which ones he'd print. Still, he barely glanced at them, leaving them hanging as he unlocked the darkroom door and stepped out. Tomorrow his outlook would be fresher. Waiting was an advantage he hadn't always had. Right now he wanted a beer. He had some thinking to do.

He headed straight for the kitchen and grabbed a cold bottle. Popping off the lid, he tossed it into the can his once-a-week housekeeper lined with plastic. The room was clean, not particularly cheerful with the hard whites and blacks, but then it wasn't dull.

After he tilted the bottle back, he chugged the beer down, draining half. He lit a cigarette, then took the beer to the kitchen table where he leaned back in a chair and propped his feet on the scrubbed wood surface.

The view out the kitchen window was of a not so glamorous L.A. It was a little seamy, rough, sturdy and tough. The early evening light couldn't make it pretty. He could've moved to a glossier part of town, or out to the hills where the lights of the city at night looked like a fairy tale. Shade preferred the small apartment that looked out over the umpampered streets of a city known for glitz. He didn't have much patience with glitz.

Bryan Mitchell. She specialized in it.

He couldn't deny that her portraits of the rich, famous and beautiful were well done—even excellent ones of their kind. There was compassion in her photographs, humor and a smooth sensuality. He wouldn't even deny that there was a place for her kind of work in the field. It just wasn't his angle. She reflected culture, he went straight for life.

Her work for *Celebrity* magazine had been professional, slick and often searing in its way. The larger-than-life people she'd photographed had often been cut down to size in a way that made them human and approachable. Since she'd decided to free-lance, the stars, near stars and star makers she'd photographed for the glossy came to her. Over the years, she'd developed a reputation and style that had made her one of them, part of the inner, select circle.

It could happen to a photographer, he knew. They could come to resemble their own themes, their own studies. Sometimes what they tried to project became a part of them. Too much a part. No, he didn't begrudge

Bryan Mitchell her state of the art. Shade simply had doubts about working with her.

He didn't care for partnerships.

Yet those were the terms. When he'd been approached by *Life-style* to do a pictorial study of America, he'd been intrigued. Photo essays could make a strong, lasting statement that could rock and jar or soothe and amuse. As a photographer, he had sought to do that. *Life-style* wanted him, wanted the strong, sometimes concise, sometimes ambiguous emotions his pictures could portray. But they also wanted a counterbalance. A woman's view.

He wasn't so stubborn that he didn't see the point and the possibilities. Yet it irked him to think that the assignment hinged on his willingness to share the summer, his van and the credit with a celebrity photographer. And with a woman at that. Three months on the road with a female who spent her time perfecting snapshots of rock stars and personalities. For a man who'd cut his professional teeth in war-torn Lebanon, it didn't sound like a picnic.

But he wanted to do it. He wanted the chance to capture an American summer from L.A. to New York, showing the joy, the pathos, the sweat, the cheers and disappointments. He wanted to show the heart even while he stripped it to the bone.

All he had to do was say yes, and share the summer with Bryan Mitchell.

"Don't think about the camera, Maria. Dance." Bryan lined up the forty-year-old ballet superstar in her viewfinder. She liked what she saw. Age? Touches of it, but years meant nothing. Grit, style, elegance. Endurance—

most of all, endurance. Bryan knew how to catch them all and meld them.

Maria Natravidova had been photographed countless times over her phenomenal twenty-five-year career. But never with sweat running down her arms and dampening her leotard. Never with the strain showing. Bryan wasn't looking for the illusions dancers live with, but the exhaustion, the aches that were the price of triumph.

She caught Maria in a leap, legs stretched parallel to the floor, arms flung wide in perfect alignment. Drops of moisture danced from her face and shoulders; muscles bunched and held. Bryan pressed the shutter, then moved the camera slightly to blur the motion.

That would be the one. She knew it even as she finished off the roll of film.

"You make me work," the dancer complained as she slid into a chair, blotting her streaming face with a towel.

Bryan took two more shots, then lowered her camera. "I could've dressed you in costume, backlit you and had you hold an arabesque. That would show that you're beautiful, graceful. Instead I'm going to show that you're a strong woman."

"And you're a clever one." Maria sighed as she let the towel drop. "Why else do I come to you for the pictures for my book?"

"Because I'm the best." Bryan crossed the studio and disappeared into a back room. Maria systematically worked a cramp out of her calf. "Because I understand you, admire you. And—" she brought out a tray, two glasses and a pitcher clinking with ice "—because I squeeze oranges for you."

"Darling." With a laugh, Maria reached for the first glass. For a moment, she held it to her high forehead, then drank deeply. Her dark hair was pulled back severely in a style only good bones and flawless skin could tolerate. Stretching out her long, thin body in the chair, she studied Bryan over the rim of her glass.

Maria had known Bryan for seven years, since the photographer had started at *Celebrity* with the assignment to take pictures of the dancer backstage. The dancer had been a star, but Bryan hadn't shown awe. Maria could still remember the young woman with the thick honey-colored braid and bib overalls. The elegant prima ballerina had found herself confronted with candid eyes the color of pewter, an elegant face with slanting cheekbones and a full mouth. The tall, athletic body had nearly been lost inside the baggy clothes. She'd worn ragged sneakers and long, dangling earrings.

Maria glanced down at the dingy Nikes Bryan wore. Some things didn't change. At first glance, you'd categorize the tall, tanned blonde in sneakers and shorts as typically California. Looks could be deceiving. There was nothing typical about Bryan Mitchell.

Bryan accepted the stare as she drank. "What do you see, Maria?" It interested her to know. Conceptions and preconceptions were part of her trade.

"A strong, smart woman with talent and ambition." Maria smiled as she leaned back in the chair. "Myself, nearly."

Bryan smiled. "A tremendous compliment."

Maria acknowledged this with a sweeping gesture. "There aren't many women I like. Myself I like, and so, you. I hear rumors, my love, about you and that pretty young actor."

"Matt Perkins." Bryan didn't believe in evading or pretending. She lived, by choice, in a town fueled by rumors, fed by gossip. "I took his picture, had a few dinners."

"Nothing serious?"

"As you said, he's pretty." Bryan smiled and chewed on a piece of ice. "But there's barely room enough for his ego and mine in his Mercedes."

"Men." Maria leaned forward to pour herself a second glass.

"Now you're going to be profound."

"Who better?" Maria countered. "Men." She said the word again, savoring it. "I find them tedious, childish, foolish and indispensable. Being loved . . . sexually, you understand?"

Bryan managed to keep her lips from curving. "I understand."

"Being loved is exhilarating, exhausting. Like Christmas. Sometimes I feel like the child who doesn't understand why Christmas ends. But it does. And you wait for the next time."

It always fascinated Bryan how people felt about love, how they dealt with it, groped for it and avoided it. "Is that why you never married, Maria? You're waiting for the next time?"

"I married dance. To marry a man I would have to divorce dance. There's no room for two for a woman like me. And you?"

Bryan stared into her drink, no longer amused. She understood the words too well. "No room for two," she murmured. "But I don't wait for the next time."

"You're young. If you could have Christmas every day, would you turn away from it?"

Bryan moved her shoulders. "I'm too lazy for Christmas every day."

"Still, it's a pretty fantasy." Maria rose and stretched. "You've made me work long enough. I have to shower and change. Dinner with my choreographer."

Alone, Bryan absently ran a finger over the back of her camera. She didn't often think about love and marriage. She'd been there already. Once a fantasy was exposed to reality it faded, like a photo improperly fixed. Permanent relationships rarely worked, and still more rarely worked well.

She thought of Lee Radcliffe, married to Hunter Brown for nearly a year, helping to raise his daughter and pregnant with her first child. Lee was happy, but then she'd found an extraordinary man, one who wanted her to be what she was, even encouraged her to explore herself. Bryan's own experience had taught her that what's said and what's felt can be two opposing things.

Your career's as important to me as it is to you. How many times had Rob said that *before* they'd been married? *Get your degree. Go for it.*

So they'd gotten married, young, eager, idealistic. Within six months he'd been unhappy with the time she'd put into her classes and her job at a local studio. He'd wanted his dinner hot and his socks washed. Not so much to ask, Bryan mused. To be fair, she had to say that Rob had asked for little of her. Just too much at the time.

They'd cared for each other and both had tried to make adjustments. Both had discovered they'd wanted different things for themselves—different things from each other, things neither could be, neither could give.

It would've been called an amicable divorce—no fury, no bitterness. No passion. A signature on a legal document, and the dream had been over. It had hurt more than anything Bryan had ever known. The taint of failure had stayed with her a long, long time.

She knew Rob had remarried. He was living in the suburbs with his wife and their two children. He'd gotten what he'd wanted.

And so, Bryan told herself as she looked around her studio, had she. She didn't just want to be a photographer. She was a photographer. The hours she spent in the field, in her studio, in the darkroom were as essential to her as sleep. And what she'd done in the six years since the end of her marriage, she'd done on her own. She didn't have to share it. She didn't have to share her time. Perhaps she was a great deal like Maria. She was a woman who ran her own life, made her own decisions, personally and professionally. Some people weren't made for partnerships.

Shade Colby. Bryan propped her feet on Maria's chair. She might just have to make a concession there. She admired his work. So much so, in fact, that she'd plunked down a heady amount for his print of an L.A. street scene at a time when money had been a large concern. She'd studied it, trying to analyze and guess at the techniques he'd used for setting the shot and making the print. It was a moody piece, so much gray, so little light. And yet, Bryan had sensed a certain grit in it, not hopelessness, but ruthlessness. Still, admiring his work and working with him were two different things.

They were based in the same town, but they moved in different circles. For the most part, Shade Colby didn't move in any circles. He kept to himself. She'd seen him at a handful of photography functions but they'd never met.

He'd be an interesting subject, she reflected. Given enough time, she could capture that air of aloofness and earthiness on film. Perhaps if they agreed to take the assignment she'd have the chance.

Three months of travel. There was so much of the country she hadn't seen, so many pictures she hadn't taken. Thoughtfully, she pulled a candy bar out of her back pocket and unwrapped it. She liked the idea of taking a slice of America, a season, and pulling the images together. So much could be said.

Bryan enjoyed doing her portraits. Taking a face, a personality, especially a well-known one and finding out what lay behind it was fascinating. Some might find it limited, but she found it endlessly varied. She could take the tough female rock star and show her vulnerabilities, or pull the humor from the cool, regal megastar. Capturing the unexpected, the fresh—that was the purpose of photography to her.

Now she was being offered the opportunity to do the same thing with a country. The people, she thought. So many people.

She wanted to do it. If it meant sharing the work, the discoveries, the fun with Shade Colby, she still wanted to do it. She bit into the chocolate. So what if he had a reputation for being cranky and remote? She could get along with anyone for three months.

"Chocolate makes you fat and ugly."

Bryan glanced up as Maria swirled back into the room. The sweat was gone. She looked now as people expected a prima ballerina to look. Draped in silk, studded with diamonds. Cool, composed, beautiful.

"It makes me happy," Bryan countered. "You look fantastic, Maria."

"Yes." Maria brushed a hand down the draping silk at her hip. "But then it's my job to do so. Will you work late?"

"I want to develop the film. I'll send you some test proofs tomorrow."

"And that's your dinner?"

"Just a start." Bryan took a huge bite of chocolate. "I'm sending out for pizza."

"With pepperoni?"

Bryan grinned. "With everything."

Maria pressed a hand to her stomach. "And I eat with my choreographer, the tyrant, which means I eat next to nothing."

"And I'll have a soda instead of a glass of Taittinger. We all have our price to pay."

"If I like your proofs, I'll send you a case."

"Of Taittinger?"

"Of soda." With a laugh, Maria swept out.

An hour later, Bryan hung her negatives up to dry. She'd need to make the proofs to be certain, but out of more than forty shots, she'd probably print no more than five.

When her stomach rumbled, she checked her watch. She'd ordered the pizza for seven-thirty. Well timed, she decided as she left the darkroom. She'd eat and go over the prints of Matt she'd shot for a layout in a glossy. Then she could work on the one she chose until the negatives of Maria were dry. She began rummaging through the two dozen folders on her desk—her personal method of filing—when someone knocked at the studio door.

"Pizza," she breathed, greedy. "Come on in. I'm starving." Plopping her enormous canvas bag on the desk, Bryan began to hunt for her wallet. "This is great timing. Another five minutes and I might've just faded away. Shouldn't miss lunch." She dropped a fat, ragged notebook, a clear plastic bag filled with cosmetics, a key ring and five candy bars on the desk. "Just set it down anywhere, I'll find the money in a minute." She dug deeper into the bag. "How much do you need?"

"As much as I can get."

"Don't we all." Bryan pulled out a worn man's billfold. "And I'm desperate enough to clean out the safe for you, but..." She trailed off as she looked up and saw Shade Colby.

He gave her face a quick glance, then concentrated on her eyes. "What would you like to pay me for?"

"Pizza." Bryan dropped the wallet onto the desk with half the contents of her purse. "A case of starvation and mistaken identity. Shade Colby." She held out her hand, curious, and to her surprise, nervous. He looked more formidable when he wasn't in a crowd. "I recognize you," she continued, "but I don't think we've met."

"No, we haven't." He took her hand and held it while he studied her face a second time. Stronger than he'd expected. He always looked for the strength first, then the weaknesses. And younger. Though he knew she was only twenty-eight, Shade had expected her to look harder, more aggressive, glossier. Instead, she looked like someone who'd just come in from the beach.

Her T-shirt was snug, but she was slim enough to warrant it. The braid came nearly to her waist and made him speculate on how her hair would look loose and free. Her eyes interested him—gray edging toward silver and almond shaped. They were eyes he'd like to photograph with the rest of her face in shadow. She might carry a bag of cosmetics, but it didn't look as if she used any of them.

Not vain about her appearance, he decided. That would make things simpler if he decided to work with her. He didn't have the patience to wait while a woman painted and groomed and fussed. This one wouldn't. And she was assessing him even as he assessed her. Shade accepted that. A photographer, like any artist, looked for angles.

"Am I interrupting your work?"

"No, I was just taking a break. Sit down."

They were both cautious. He'd come on impulse. She wasn't certain how to handle him. Each decided to bide their time before they went beyond the polite, impersonal stage. Bryan remained behind her desk. Her turf, his move, she decided.

Shade didn't sit immediately. Instead, he tucked his hands in his pockets and looked around her studio. It was wide, well lit from the ribbon of windows. There were baby spots and a blue backdrop still set up from an earlier session in one section. Reflectors and umbrellas stood in another with a camera still on a tripod. He didn't have to look closely to see that the equipment was first-class. But then, first-class equipment didn't make a first-class photographer.

She liked the way he stood, not quite at ease, but ready, remote. If she had to choose now, she'd have photographed him in shadows, alone. But Bryan insisted on knowing the person before she made a portrait.

How old was he? she wondered. Thirty-three, thirty-five. He'd already been nominated for a Pulitzer when she'd still been in college. It didn't occur to her to be intimidated.

"Nice place," he commented before he dropped into the chair opposite the desk.

"Thanks." She tilted her chair so that she could study him from another angle. "You don't use a studio of your own, do you?"

"I work in the field." He drew out a cigarette. "On the rare occasion I need a studio I can borrow or rent one easily enough."

Automatically she hunted for an ashtray under the chaos on her desk. "You make all your own prints?"

"That's right."

Bryan nodded. On the few occasions at *Celebrity* when she'd been forced to entrust her film to someone else, she hadn't been satisfied. That had been one of the major reasons she'd decided to open her own business. "I love darkroom work."

She smiled for the first time, causing him to narrow his eyes and focus on her face. What kind of power was that? he wondered. A curving of lips, easy and relaxed. It packed one hell of a punch.

Bryan sprang up at the knock on the door. "At last."

Shade watched her cross the room. He hadn't known she was so tall. Five-ten, he estimated, and most of it leg. Long, slender, bronzed leg. It wasn't easy to ignore the smile, but it was next to impossible to ignore those legs.

Nor had he noticed her scent until she moved by him. Lazy sex. He couldn't think of another way to describe it. It wasn't floral, it wasn't sophisticated. It was basic. Shade drew on his cigarette and watched her laugh with the delivery boy.

Photographers were known for their preconceptions; it was part of the trade. He'd expected her to be sleek and cool. That was what he'd nearly resigned himself to work with. Now it was a matter of rearranging his thinking. Did he want to work with a woman who smelled like twilight and looked like a beach bunny?

Turning away from her, Shade opened a folder at random. He recognized the subject—a box-office queen with two Oscars and three husbands under her belt. Bryan had dressed her in glitters and sparkles. Royal trappings for royalty. But she hadn't shot the traditional picture.

The actress was sitting at a table jumbled with pots and tubes of lotions and creams, looking at her own reflection in a mirror and laughing. Not the poised, careful smile that didn't make wrinkles, but a full, robust laugh that could nearly be heard. It was up to the viewer to speculate whether she laughed at her reflection or an image she'd created over the years.

"Like it?" Carrying the cardboard box, Bryan stopped beside him.

"Yeah. Did she?"

Too hungry for formalities, Bryan opened the lid and dug out the first piece. "She ordered a sixteen by twenty-four for her fiancé. Want a piece?"

Shade looked inside the box. "They miss putting anything on here?"

"Nope." Bryan searched in a drawer of her desk for napkins and came up with a box of tissues. "I'm a firm believer in overindulgence. So..." With the box opened on the desk between them, Bryan leaned back in her chair and propped up her feet. It was time, she decided, to get beyond the fencing stage. "You want to talk about the assignment?"

Shade took a piece of pizza and a handful of tissues. "Got a beer?"

"Soda—diet or regular." Bryan took a huge, satisfying bite. "I don't keep liquor in the studio. You end up having buzzed clients."

"We'll skip it for now." They ate in silence a moment, still weighing each other. "I've been giving a lot of thought to doing this photo essay."

"It'd be a change for you." When he only lifted a brow, Bryan wadded a tissue and tossed it into the trash can. "Your stuff overseas—it hit hard. There was sensitivity and compassion, but for the most part, it was grim."

"It was a grim time. Everything I shoot doesn't have to be pretty."

This time she lifted a brow. Obviously he didn't think much of the path she'd taken in her career. "Everything I shoot doesn't have to be raw. There's room for fun in art."

He acknowledged this with a shrug. "We'd see different things if we looked through the same lens."

"That's what makes each picture unique." Bryan leaned forward and took another piece.

"I like working alone."

She ate thoughtfully. If he was trying to annoy her, he was right on target. If it was just an overflow of his personality, it still wouldn't make things any easier. Either way, she wanted the assignment, and he was part of it. "I prefer it that way myself," she said slowly. "Sometimes there has to be compromise. You've heard of compromise, Shade. You give, I give. We meet somewhere close to the middle."

She wasn't as laid-back as she looked. Good. The last thing he needed was to go on the road with someone so mellow she threatened to mold. Three months, he thought again. Maybe. Once the ground rules were set. "I map out the route," he began briskly. "We start here in L.A. in two weeks. Each of us is responsible for their own equipment. Once we're on the road, each of us goes our own way. You shoot your pictures, I shoot mine. No questions."

Bryan licked sauce from her finger. "Anyone ever question you, Colby?"

"It's more to the point whether I answer." It was said simply, as it was meant. "The publisher wants both views, so he'll have them. We'll be stopping off and on to rent a darkroom. I'll look over your negatives."

Bryan wadded more tissue. "No, you won't." Lazily, she crossed one ankle over the other. Her eyes had gone to slate, the only outward show of a steadily growing anger.

"I'm not interested in having my name attached to a series of pop culture shots."

To keep herself in control, Bryan continued to eat. There were things, so many clear, concise things, she'd like to say to him. Temper took a great deal of energy, she reminded herself. It usually accomplished nothing. "The first thing I'll want written into the contract is that each of our pictures carries our own bylines. That way neither of us will be embarrassed by the other's work. I'm not interested in having the public think I have no sense of humor. Want another piece?"

"No." She wasn't soft. The skin on the inside of her elbow might look soft as butter, but the lady wasn't. It might annoy him to be so casually insulted, but he preferred it to spineless agreement. "We'll be gone from June fifteenth until after Labor Day." He watched her scoop up a third piece of pizza. "Since I've seen you eat, we'll each keep track of our own expenses."

"Fine. Now, in case you have any odd ideas, I don't cook and I won't pick up after you. I'll drive my share, but I won't drive with you if you've been drinking. When we rent a darkroom, we trade off as to who uses it first. From June fifteenth to after Labor Day, we're partners. Fifty-fifty. If you have any problems with that, we'll hash it out now, before we sign on the dotted line."

He thought about it. She had a good voice, smooth, quiet, nearly soothing. They might handle the close quarters well enough—as long as she didn't smile at him too often and he kept his mind off her legs. At the moment, he considered that the least of his problems. The assignment came first and what he wanted for it, and from it.

"Do you have a lover?"

Bryan managed not to choke on her pizza. "If that's an offer," she began smoothly, "I'll have to decline. Rude, brooding men just aren't my type."

Inwardly he acknowledged another hit; outwardly his face remained expressionless. "We're going to be living in each other's pockets for three months." She'd challenged him, whether she realized it or not. Whether he realized it or not, Shade had accepted. He leaned closer. "I don't want to hassle with a jealous lover chasing along after us or constantly calling while I'm trying to work."

Just who did he think she was? Some bimbo who couldn't handle her personal life? She made herself pause a moment. Perhaps he'd had some uncomfortable experiences in his relationships. His problem, Bryan decided.

"I'll worry about my lovers, Shade." Bryan bit into her crust with a vengeance. "You worry about yours." She wiped her fingers on the last of the tissue and smiled. "Sorry to break up the party, but I've got to get back to work."

He rose, letting his gaze skim up her legs before he met her eyes. He was going to take the assignment. And he'd have three months to figure out just how he felt about Bryan Mitchell. "I'll be in touch."

"Do that."

Bryan waited until he'd crossed the room and shut the studio door behind him. With uncommon energy, and a speed she usually reserved for work, she jumped up and tossed the empty cardboard box at the door.

It promised to be a long three months.

Chapter Two

She knew exactly what she wanted. Bryan might've been a bit ahead of the scheduled starting date for the American Summer project for *Life-style*, but she enjoyed the idea of being a step ahead of Shade Colby. Petty perhaps, but she did enjoy it.

In any case, she doubted a man like him would appreciate the timeless joy of the last day of school. When else did summer really start but with that one wild burst of freedom?

She chose an elementary school because she wanted innocence. She chose an inner city school because she wanted realism. Children who would step out the door and into a limo weren't the image she wanted to project. This school could've been in any city across the country. The kids who'd bolt out the door would be all kids. People who looked at the photograph, no matter what their age, would see something of themselves.

Bryan gave herself plenty of time to set up, choosing and rejecting a half a dozen vantage points before she settled on one. It wasn't possible or even advisable to stage the shoot. Only random shots would give her what she wanted—the spontaneity and the rush.

When the bell rang and the doors burst open, she got exactly that. It was well worth nearly being trampled under flying sneakers. With shouts and yells and whistles, kids poured out into the sunshine.

Stampede. That was the thought that went through her mind. Crouching quickly, Bryan shot up, catching the first rush of children at an angle that would convey speed, mass and total confusion.

Let's go, let's go! It's summer and every day's Saturday. September was years away. She could read it on the face of every child.

Turning, she shot the next group of children head-on. In the finished spot they'd appear to be charging right out of the page of the magazine. On impulse, she shifted her camera for a vertical shot. And she got it. A boy of eight or nine leaped down the flight of steps, hands flung high, a grin splitting his face. Bryan shot him in midair while he hung head and shoulders above the scattering children. She'd captured the boy filled with the triumph of that magic, golden road of freedom spreading out in all directions.

Though she was dead sure which shot she'd print for the assignment, Bryan continued to work. Within ten minutes, it was over.

Satisfied, she changed lenses and angles. The school was empty now, and she wanted to record it that way. She didn't want the feel of bright sunlight here, she decided as she added a low contrast filter. When she developed the print, Bryan would "dodge" the light in the sky by holding something over that section of the paper to keep it from being overexposed. She wanted the sense of emptiness, of waiting, as a contrast to the life and energy that had just poured out of the building. She'd exhausted a roll of film before she straightened and let the camera hang by its strap.

School's out, she thought with a grin. She felt that charismatic pull of freedom herself. Summer was just beginning.

* * *

Since resigning from the staff of *Celebrity*, Bryan found her work load hadn't eased. If anything, she'd found herself to be a tougher employer than the magazine. She loved her work and was likely to give it all of her day and most of her evenings. Her ex-husband had once accused her of being obsessed not with her camera, but by it. It was something she'd neither been able to deny nor defend. After two days of working with Shade, Bryan discovered she wasn't alone.

She'd always considered herself a meticulous craftsman. Compared to Shade, she was lackadaisical. He had a patience in his work she admired even as it set her teeth on edge. They worked from entirely different perspectives. Bryan shot a scene and conveyed her personal viewpoint—her emotions, her feelings about the image. Shade deliberately courted ambiguity. While his photographs might spark off a dozen varied reactions, his personal view almost always remained his secret. Just as everything about him remained half shadowed.

He didn't chat, but Bryan didn't mind working in silence. It was nearly like working alone. His long, quiet looks could be unnerving, however. She didn't care to be dissected as though she were in a viewfinder.

They'd met twice since their first encounter in her studio, both times to argue out their basic route and the themes for the assignment. She hadn't found him any easier, but she had found him sharp. The project meant enough to both of them to make it possible for them to do as she'd suggested—meet somewhere in the middle.

After her initial annoyance with him had worn off, Bryan had decided they could become friends over the next months—professional friends, in any case. Then after two days of working with him, she knew it would never happen. Shade didn't induce simple emotions like friendship. He'd either dazzle or infuriate. She didn't choose to be dazzled.

Bryan had researched him thoroughly, telling herself her reason was routine. You didn't go on the road with a man you knew virtually nothing about. Yet the more she'd found out—rather the more she hadn't found out—the deeper her curiosity had become.

He'd been married and divorced in his early twenties. That was it—no anecdotes, no gossip, no right and wrong. He covered his tracks well. As a photographer for *International View*, Shade had spent a total of five years overseas. Not in pretty Paris, London and Madrid, but in Laos, Lebanon, Cambodia. His work there had earned him a Pulitzer nomination and the Overseas Press Club Award.

His photographs were available for study and dissection, but his personal life remained obscure. He socialized rarely. What friends he had were unswervingly loyal and frustratingly close-mouthed. If she wanted to learn more about him, Bryan would have to do it on the job.

Bryan considered the fact that they'd agreed to spend their last day in L.A. working at the beach a good sign. They'd decided on the location without any argument. Beach scenes would be an ongoing theme throughout the essay—California to Cape Cod.

At first they walked along the sand together, like friends or lovers, not touching but in step with each other. They didn't talk, but Bryan had already learned that Shade didn't make idle conversation unless he was in the mood.

It was barely ten, but the sun was bright and hot. Because it was a weekday morning, most of the sun and water seekers were the young or the old. When Bryan stopped, Shade kept walking without either of them saying a word.

It was the contrast that had caught her eye. The old woman was bundled in a wide, floppy sun hat, a long beach dress and a crocheted shawl. She sat under an umbrella and watched her granddaughter—dressed only in frilly pink panties—dig a hole in the sand beside her. Sun poured over the little girl. Shade blanketed the old woman.

She'd need the woman to sign a release form. Invariably, asking someone if you could take her picture stiffened her up, and Bryan avoided it whenever it was possible. In this case it wasn't, so she was patient enough to chat and wait until the woman had relaxed again.

Her name was Sadie, and so was her granddaughter's. Before she'd clicked the shutter the first time, Bryan knew she'd title the print *Two Sadies*. All she had to do was get that dreamy, faraway look back in the woman's eyes.

It took twenty minutes. Bryan forgot she was uncomfortably warm as she listened, thought and reasoned out the angles. She knew what she wanted. The old woman's careful self-preservation, the little girl's total lack of it and the bond between them that came with blood and time.

Lost in reminiscence, Sadie forgot about the camera, not noticing when Bryan began to release the shutter. She wanted the poignancy—that's what she'd seen. When she printed it, Bryan would be merciless with the lines and creases in the grandmother's face, just as she'd highlight the flawlessness of the toddler's skin.

Grateful, Bryan chatted a few more minutes, then noted the woman's address with the promise of a print. She walked on, waiting for the next scene to unfold.

Shade had his first subject as well, but he didn't chat. The man lay facedown on a faded beach towel. He was red, flabby and anonymous. A businessman taking the morning off, a salesman from Iowa—it didn't matter. Unlike Bryan, he wasn't looking for personality but for the sameness of those who grilled their bodies under the sun. There was a plastic bottle of tanning lotion stuck in the sand beside him and a pair of rubber beach thongs.

Shade chose two angles and shot six times without exchanging a word with the snoring sunbather. Satisfied, he scanned the beach. Three yards away, Bryan was casually stripping out of her shorts and shirt. The sleek red maillot rose tantalizing high at the thighs. Her profile was to him as she stepped out of her shorts. It was sharp, well defined, like something sculpted with a meticulous hand.

Shade didn't hesitate. He focused her in his viewfinder, set the aperture, adjusted the angle no more than a fraction and waited. At the moment when she reached down for the hem of her T-shirt he began to shoot.

She was so easy, so unaffected. He'd forgotten anyone could be so totally unself-conscious in a world where self-absorption had become a religion. Her body was one long lean line, with more and more exposed as she drew the shirt over her head. For a moment, she tilted her face up to the sun, inviting the heat. Something crawled into his stomach and began to twist, slowly.

Desire. He recognized it. He didn't care for it.

It was, he could tell himself, what was known in the trade as a decisive moment. The photographer thinks, then shoots, while watching the unfolding scene. When the visual and the emotional elements come together—as they had in this case with a punch—there was success. There were no replays here, no reshooting. Decisive moment meant exactly that, all or nothing. If he'd been shaken for a instant, it only proved he'd been successful in capturing that easy, lazy sexuality.

Years before he'd trained himself not to become overly emotional about his subjects. They could eat you alive. Bryan Mitchell might not look as though she'd take a bite out of a man, but Shade didn't take chances. He turned away from her and forgot her. Almost.

It was more than four hours later before their paths crossed again. Bryan sat in the sun near a concession stand eating a hot dog buried under mounds of mustard and relish. On one side of her she'd set her camera bag, on the other a can of soda. Her narrow red sunglasses shot his reflection back at him.

"How'd it go?" she asked with her mouth full.

"All right. Is there a hot dog under that?"

"Mmm." She swallowed and gestured toward the stand. "Terrific."

"I'll pass." Reaching down, Shade picked up her warming soda and took a long pull. It was orange and sweet. "How the hell do you drink this stuff?"

"I need a lot of sugar. I got some shots I'm pretty pleased with." She held out a hand for the can. "I want to make prints before we leave tomorrow."

"As long as you're ready at seven."

Bryan wrinkled her nose as she finished off her hot dog. She'd rather work until 7:00 A.M. than get up that early. One of the first things they'd have to iron out on the road was the difference in their biological schedules. She understood the beauty and power of a sunrise shot. She just happened to prefer the mystery and color of sunset.

"I'll be ready." Rising, she brushed sand off her bottom, then pulled her T-shirt over her suit. Shade could've told her she was more modest without it. The way the hem skimmed along her thighs and drew the eyes to them was nearly criminal. "As long as you drive the first shift," she continued. "By ten I'll be functional."

He didn't know why he did it. Shade was a man who analyzed each movement, every texture, shape, color. He cut everything into patterns, then reassembled them. That was his way. Impulse wasn't. Yet he reached out and curled his fingers around her braid without thinking of the act or the consequences. He just wanted to touch.

She was surprised, he could see. But she didn't pull away. Nor did she give him that small half smile women used when a man couldn't resist touching what attracted him.

Her hair was soft; his eyes had told him that but now his fingers confirmed it. Still, it was frustrating not to feel it loose and free, not to be able to let it play between his fingers.

He didn't understand her. Yet. She made her living recording the elite, the glamorous, the ostentatious, yet she seemed to have no pretensions. Her only jewelry was a thin gold chain that fell to her breasts. On the end was a tiny ankh. Again, she wore no makeup but her scent was there to tantalize. She could, with a few basic female touches, have turned herself into something breathtaking, but she seemed to ignore the possibilities and rely on simplicity. That in itself was stunning.

Hours before, Bryan had decided she didn't want to be dazzled. Shade was deciding at that moment he didn't care to be stunned. Without a word, he let her braid fall back to her shoulder.

"Do you want me to take you back to your apartment or your studio?"

So that was it? He'd managed to tie her up in knots in a matter of seconds and now he only wanted to know where to dump her off. "The studio." Bryan reached down and picked up her camera bag. Her throat was dry, but she tossed the half-full can of soda into the trash. She wasn't certain she could swallow. Before they'd reached Shade's car, she was certain she'd explode if she didn't say something.

"Do you enjoy that cool, remote image you've perfected, Shade?"

He didn't look at her, but he nearly smiled. "It's comfortable."

"Except for the people who get within five feet of you." Damned if she wouldn't get a rise out of him. "Maybe you take your own press too seriously," she suggested. "Shade Colby, as mysterious and intriguing as his name, as dangerous and as compelling as his photographs."

This time he did smile, surprising her. Abruptly he looked like someone she'd want to link hands with, laugh with. "Where in hell did you read that?"

"*Celebrity*," she muttered. "April, five years ago. They did an article on the photo sales in New York. One of your prints sold for seventy-five hundred at Sotheby's."

"Did it?" His gaze slid over her profile. "You've a better memory than I."

Stopping, she turned to face him. "Damn it, I bought it. It's a moody, depressing, fascinating street scene that I wouldn't have given ten cents for if I'd met you first. And if I wasn't so hooked on it, I'd pitch it out the minute I get home. As it is I'll probably have to turn it to face the wall for six months until I forget that the artist behind it is a jerk."

Shade watched her soberly, then nodded. "You make quite a speech once you're rolling."

With one short, rude word Bryan turned and started toward the car again. As she reached the passenger side and yanked open the door, Shade stopped her. "Since we're essentially going to be living together for the next three months, you might want to get the rest of it out now."

Though she tried to speak casually, it came out between her teeth. "The rest of what?"

"Whatever griping you have to do."

She took a deep breath first. She hated to be angry. Invariably it exhausted her. Resigned to it, Bryan curled her hands around the top of the door and leaned toward him. "I don't like you. I'd say it's just that simple, but I can't think of anyone else I don't like."

"No one?"

"No one."

For some reason he believed her. He nodded, then dropped his hands over hers on top of the door. "I'd rather not be lumped in a group in any case. Why should we have to like each other?"

"It'd make the assignment easier."

He considered this while holding her hands beneath his. The tops of hers were soft, the palms of his hard. He liked the contrast, perhaps too much. "You like things easy?"

He made it sound like an insult and she straightened. Her eyes were on a level with his mouth and she shifted slightly. "Yes. Complications are just that. They get in the way and muck things up. I'd rather shovel them aside and deal with what's important."

"We've had a major complication before we started."

She might've concentrated on keeping her eyes on his, but that didn't prevent her from feeling the light, firm pressure of his hands. It didn't prevent her from understanding his meaning. Since it was something they'd meticulously avoided mentioning from the beginning, Bryan lunged at it, straight on.

"You're a man and I'm a woman."

He couldn't help but enjoy the way she snarled it at him. "Exactly. We can say we're both photographers and that's a sexless term." He gave her the barest hint of a smile. "It's also bullshit."

"That may be," she said evenly. "But I intend to handle it because the assignment comes first. It helps a great deal that I don't like you."

"Liking doesn't have anything to do with chemistry."

She gave him an easy smile because her pulse was beginning to pound. "Is that a polite word for lust?"

She wasn't one to dance around an issue once she'd opened it up. Fair enough, he decided. "Whatever you call it, it goes right back to your complication. We'd better take a good look at it, then shove it aside."

When his fingers tightened on hers, she dropped her gaze to them. She understood his meaning, but not his reason.

"Wondering what it would be like's going to distract both of us," Shade continued. She looked up again, wary. He could feel her pulse throb where his fingers brushed her wrist, yet she'd made no move to pull back. If she had ... There was no use speculating; it was better to move ahead. "We'll find out. Then we'll file it, forget it and get on with our job."

It sounded logical. Bryan had a basic distrust of anything that sounded quite so logical. Still, he'd been right on target when he'd said that wondering would be distracting. She'd been wondering for days. His mouth seemed to be the softest thing about him, yet even that looked hard, firm and unyielding. How would it feel? How would it taste?

She let her gaze wander back to it and the lips curved. She wasn't certain if it was amusement or sarcasm, but it made up her mind.

"All right." How intimate could a kiss be when a car door separated them?

They leaned toward each other slowly, as if each waited for the other to draw back at the last moment. Their lips met lightly, passionlessly. It could've ended then with each of them shrugging the other off in disinterest. It was the basic definition of a kiss. Two pairs of lips meeting. Nothing more.

Neither one would be able to say who changed it, whether it was calculated or accidental. They were both curious people, and curiosity might have been the factor. Or it might have been inevitable. The texture of the kiss changed so slowly that it wasn't possible to stop it until it was too late for regrets.

Lips opened, invited, accepted. Their fingers clung. His head tilted, and hers, so that the kiss deepened. Bryan found herself pressing against the hard, unyielding door, searching for more, demanding it as her teeth nipped at his bottom lip. She'd been right. His mouth was the softest thing about him. Impossibly soft, unreasonably luxurious as it heated on hers.

She wasn't used to wild swings of mood. She'd never experienced anything like it. It wasn't possible to lie back and enjoy. Wasn't that what kisses were for? Up to now she'd believed so. This one demanded all her strength, all her energy. Even as it went on, she knew when it ended she'd be drained. Wonderfully, totally drained. While she reveled in the excitement, she could anticipate the glory of the aftermath.

He should've known. Damn it, he should've known she wasn't as easy and uncomplicated as she looked. Hadn't he looked at her and ached? Tasting her wasn't going to alleviate any of it, only heighten it. She could undermine his control, and control was essential to his art, his life, his sanity. He'd developed and perfected it over years of sweat, fear and expectations. Shade had learned that the same calculated control he used in the darkroom, the same careful logic he used to set a shot, could be applied to a woman successfully. Painlessly. One taste of Bryan and he realized just how tenuous control could be.

To prove to himself, perhaps to her, that he could deal with it, he allowed the kiss to deepen, grow darker, moister. Danger hovered and perhaps he courted it.

He might lose himself in the kiss, but when it was over, it would be over, and nothing would be changed.

She tasted hot, sweet, strong. She made him burn. He had to hold back or the burn would leave a scar. He had enough of them. Life wasn't as lovely as a first kiss on a hot afternoon. He knew better than most.

Shade drew away, satisfying himself that his control was still in place. Perhaps his pulse wasn't steady, his mind not perfectly clear, but he had control.

Bryan was reeling. If he'd asked her a question, any question, she'd have had no answer. Bracing herself against the car door, she waited for her equilibrium to return. She'd known the kiss would drain her. Even now, she could feel her energy flag.

He saw the look in her eyes, the soft look any man would have to struggle to resist. Shade turned away from it. "I'll drop you at the studio."

As he walked around the car to his side, Bryan dropped down on the seat. File it and forget it, she thought. Fat chance.

She tried. Bryan put so much effort into forgetting what Shade had made her feel that she worked until 3:00 A.M. By the time she'd dragged herself back to her apartment, she'd developed the film from the school and the beach, chosen the negatives she wanted to print and had perfected two of them into what she considered some of her best work.

Now she had four hours to eat, pack and sleep. After building herself an enormous sandwich, Bryan took out the one suitcase she'd been allotted for the trip and tossed in the essentials. Groggy with fatigue, she washed down bread, meat and cheese with a great gulp of milk. None of it felt too steady on her stomach, so she left her partially eaten dinner on the bedside table and went back to her packing.

She rummaged in the top of her closet for the box with the prim, man-tailored pajamas her mother had given her for Christmas. Definitely essential, she decided as she dropped them in among the disordered pile of lingerie and jeans. They were sexless, Bryan mused. She could only hope she felt sexless in them. That afternoon she'd been forcibly reminded that she was a woman, and a woman had some vulnerabilities that couldn't always be defended.

She didn't want to feel like a woman around Shade again. It was too perilous, and she avoided perilous situations. Since she wasn't the type to make a point of her femininity there should be no problem.

She told herself.

Once they were started on the assignment, they'd be so wound up in it that they wouldn't notice if the other had two heads and four thumbs.

She told herself.

What had happened that afternoon was simply one of those fleeting moments the photographer sometimes came across when the moment dictated the scene. It wouldn't happen again because the circumstances would never be the same.

She told herself.

And then she was finished thinking of Shade Colby. It was nearly four, and the next three hours were all hers, the last she had left to herself for a long time. She'd spend them the way she liked best. Asleep. Stripping, Bryan let her clothes fall in a heap, then crawled into bed without remembering to turn off the light.

Across town, Shade lay in the dark. He hadn't slept, although he'd been packed for hours. His bag and his equipment were neatly stacked at the door. He was organized, prepared and wide awake.

He'd lost sleep before. The fact didn't concern him, but the reason did. Bryan Mitchell. Though he'd managed to push her to the side, to the back, to the corner of his mind throughout the evening, he couldn't quite get her out.

He could dissect what had happened between them that afternoon point by point, but it didn't change one essential thing. He'd been vulnerable. Perhaps only for an instant, only a heartbeat, but he'd been vulnerable. That was something he couldn't afford. It was something he wouldn't allow to happen a second time.

Bryan Mitchell was one of the complications she claimed she liked to avoid. He, on the other hand, was used to them. He'd never had any problem dealing with complications. She'd be no different.

He told himself.

For the next three months they'd be deep into a project that should totally involve all their time and energy. When he worked, he was well able to channel his concentration on one point and ignore everything else. That was no problem.

He told himself.

What had happened had happened. He still believed it was best done away with before they started out—best that they did away with the speculation and the tension it could cause. They'd eliminated the tension.

He told himself.

But he couldn't sleep. The ache in his stomach had nothing to do with the dinner that had grown cold on his plate, untouched.

He had three hours to himself, then he'd have three months of Bryan. Closing his eyes, Shade did what he was always capable of doing under stress. He willed himself to sleep.

Chapter Three

Bryan was up and dressed by seven, but she wasn't ready to talk to anyone. She had her suitcase and tripod in one hand, with two camera bags and her purse slung crosswise over her shoulders. As Shade pulled up to the curb, she was walking down the stairs and onto the sidewalk. She believed in being prompt, but not necessarily cheerful.

She grunted to Shade; it was as close to a greeting as she could manage at that hour. In silence, she loaded her gear into his van, then kicked back in the passenger seat, stretched out her legs and closed her eyes.

Shade looked at what he could see of her face behind round amber-lensed sunglasses and under a battered straw hat. "Rough night?" he asked, but she was already asleep. Shaking his head, he released the brake and pulled out into the street. They were on their way.

Shade didn't mind long drives. It gave him a chance to think or not think as he chose. In less than an hour, he was out of L.A. traffic and heading northeast on the interstate. He liked riding into the rising sun with a clear road ahead. Light bounced off the chrome on the van, shimmered on the hood and sliced down on the road signs.

He planned to cover five or six hundred miles that day, leading up toward Utah, unless something interesting caught his eye and they stopped for a shoot. After this first day, he saw no reason for them to be mileage crazy. It would hamper the point of the assignment. They'd drive as they needed to, working toward and around the definite destinations they'd ultimately agreed on.

He had a route that could easily be altered, and no itinerary. Their only time frame was to be on the east coast by Labor Day. He turned the radio on low and found some gritty country music as he drove at a steady mile-eating pace. Beside him, Bryan slept.

If this was her routine, he mused, they wouldn't have any problems. As long as she was asleep, they couldn't grate on each other's nerves. Or stir each other's passion. Even now he wondered why thoughts of her had kept him restless throughout the night. What was it about her that had worried him? He didn't know, and that was a worry in itself.

Shade liked to be able to put his finger on things and pick a problem apart until the pieces were small enough to rearrange to his preference. Even though she was quiet, almost unobtrusive at the moment, he didn't believe he'd be able to do that with Bryan Mitchell.

After his decision to take the assignment he'd made it his business to find out more about her. Shade might guard his personal life and snarl over his privacy, but he wasn't at a loss for contacts. He'd known of her work for *Celebrity*, and her more inventive and personalized work for magazines like *Vanity* and *In Touch*. She'd developed into something of a cult artist over the years with her offbeat, often radical photographs of the famous.

What he hadn't known was that she was the daughter of a painter and a poet, both eccentric and semisuccessful residents of Carmel. She'd been married to an accountant before she'd been twenty and had divorced him three years later. She dated with an almost studied casualness, and she had vague plans about buying a beach house at Malibu. She was well liked, respected, and by all accounts, dependable. She was often slow in doing things—a combination of her need for perfection and her belief that rushing was a waste of energy.

He'd found nothing surprising in his research, nor any clue as to his attraction to her. But a photographer, a successful one, was patient. Sometimes it was necessary to come back to a subject again and again until you understood your own emotion toward it.

As they crossed the border into Nevada, Shade lit a cigarette and rolled down his window. Bryan stirred, grumbled, then groped for her bag.

"Morning." Shade sent her a brief, sidelong look.

"Mmm-hmm." Bryan rooted through the bag, then gripped the chocolate bar in relief. With two quick rips she unwrapped it and tossed the trash in her purse. She usually cleaned it out before it overflowed.

"You always eat candy for breakfast?"

"Caffeine." She took a huge bite and sighed. "I prefer mine this way." Slowly, she stretched, torso, shoulders, arms, in one long, sinuous move that was completely unplanned. It was, Shade thought ironically, one definitive clue as to the attraction. "So where are we?"

"Nevada." He blew out a stream of smoke that whipped out the open window. "Just."

Bryan folded her legs under her as she nibbled on the candy bar. "It must be about my shift."

"I'll let you know."

"Okay." She was content to ride as long as he was content to drive. She did, however, give a meaningful glance at the radio. Country music wasn't her style. "Driver picks the tunes."

He shrugged his acceptance. "If you want to wash that candy down with something, there's some juice in a jug in the back."

"Yeah?" Always interested in putting something into her stomach, Bryan unfolded herself and worked her way into the back of the van.

She hadn't paid any attention to the van that morning, except for a bleary scan that told her it was black and well cared for. There were padded benches along each side that could, if you weren't too choosy, be suitable for beds. Bryan thought the pewter carpet might be the better choice.

Shade's equipment was neatly secured, and hers was loaded haphazardly into a corner. Above, glossy ebony cabinets held some essentials. Coffee, a hot plate, a small teakettle. They'd come in handy, she thought, if they stopped in any campgrounds with electric hookups. In the meantime, she settled for the insulated jug of juice.

"Want some?"

He glanced in the rearview mirror to see her standing, legs spread for balance, one hand resting on the cabinet. "Yeah."

Bryan took two jumbo Styrofoam cups and the jug back to her seat. "All the comforts of home," she commented with a jerk of her head toward the back. "Do you travel in this much?"

"When it's necessary." He heard the ice thump against the Styrofoam and held out his hand. "I don't like to fly. You lose any chance you'd have at getting a shot at something on the way." After flipping his cigarette out the window, he drank his juice. "If it's an assignment within five hundred miles or so, I drive."

"I hate to fly." Bryan propped herself in the V between the seat and the door. "It seems I'm forever hav-

ing to fly to New York to photograph someone who can't
or won't come to me. I take a bottle of Dramamine, a
supply of chocolate bars, a rabbit's foot and a socially
significant, educational book. It covers all the bases.''

''The Dramamine and the rabbit's foot maybe.''

''The chocolate's for my nerves. I like to eat when I'm
tense. The book's a bargaining point.'' She shook her
glass so the ice clinked. ''I feel like I'm saying—see, I'm
doing something worthwhile here. Let's not mess it up by
crashing the plane. Then too, the book usually puts me
to sleep within twenty minutes.''

The corner of Shade's mouth lifted, something Bryan
took as a hopeful sign for the several thousand miles they
had to go. ''That explains it.''

''I have a phobia about flying at thirty thousand feet
in a heavy tube of metal with two hundred strangers,
many of whom like to tell the intimate details of their
lives to the person next to them.'' Propping her feet on
the dash, she grinned. ''I'd rather drive across country
with one cranky photographer who makes it a point to
tell me as little as possible.''

Shade sent her a sidelong look and decided there was
no harm in playing the game as long as they both knew
the rules. ''You haven't asked me anything.''

''Okay, we'll start with something basic. Where'd
Shade come from? The name, I mean.''

He slowed down, veering off toward a rest stop.
''Shadrach.''

Her eyes widened in appreciation. ''As in Meshach and
Abednego in the Book of Daniel?''

''That's right. My mother decided to give each of her
offspring a name that would roll around a bit. I've a sister named Cassiopeia. Why Bryan?''

''My parents wanted to show they weren't sexist.''

The minute the van stopped in a parking space, Bryan hopped out, bent from the waist and touched her palms to the asphalt—much to the interest of the man climbing in the Pontiac next to her. With the view fuddling his concentration, it took him a full thirty seconds to fit his key in the ignition.

"God, I get so stiff!" She stretched up, standing on her toes, then dropped down again. "Look, there's a snack bar over there. I'm going to get some fries. Want some?"

"It's ten o'clock in the morning."

"Almost ten-thirty," she corrected. "Besides, people eat hash browns for breakfast. What's the difference?"

He was certain there was one, but didn't feel like a debate. "You go ahead. I want to buy a paper."

"Fine." As an afterthought, Bryan climbed back inside and grabbed her camera. "I'll meet you back here in ten minutes."

Her intentions were good, but she took nearly twenty. Even as she'd approached the snack bar, the formation of the line of people waiting for fast food caught her imagination. There were perhaps ten people wound out like a snake in front of a sign that read Eat Qwik.

They were dressed in baggy bermudas, wrinkled sundresses and cotton pants. A curvy teenager had on a pair of leather shorts that looked as though they'd been painted on. A woman six back from the stand fanned herself with a wide-brimmed hat banded with a floaty ribbon.

They were all going somewhere, all waiting to get there, and none of them paid any attention to anyone else. Bryan couldn't resist. She walked up the line one way, down it another until she found her angle.

She shot them from the back so that the line seemed elongated and disjointed and the sign loomed promisingly. The man behind the counter serving food was nothing more than a vague shadow that might or might not have been there. She'd taken more than her allotted ten minutes before she joined the line herself.

Shade was leaning against the van reading the paper when she returned. He'd already taken three calculated shots of the parking lot, focusing on a line of cars with license plates from five different states. When he glanced up, Bryan had her camera slung over her shoulder, a giant chocolate shake in one hand and a jumbo order of fries smothered in ketchup in the other.

"Sorry." She dipped into the box of fries as she walked. "I got a couple of good shots of the line at the snack bar. Half of summer's hurry up and wait, isn't it?"

"Can you drive with all that?"

"Sure." She swung into the driver's side. "I'm used to it." She balanced the shake between her thighs, settled the fries just ahead of it and reached out a hand for the keys.

Shade glanced down at the breakfast snuggled between very smooth, very brown legs. "Still willing to share?"

Bryan turned her head to check the rearview as she backed out. "Nope." She gave the wheel a quick turn and headed toward the exit. "You had your chance." With one competent hand steering, she dug into the fries again.

"You eat like that, you should have acne down to your navel."

"Myths," she announced and zoomed past a slower-moving sedan. With a few quick adjustments she had an old Simon and Garfunkel tune pouring out of the radio. "That's music," she told him. "I like songs that give me a visual. Country music's usually about hurting and cheating and drinking."

"And life."

Bryan picked up her shake and drew on the straw. "Maybe. I guess I get tired of too much reality. Your work depends on it."

"And yours often skirts around it."

Her brows knit, then she deliberately relaxed. In his way, he was right. "Mine gives options. Why'd you take this assignment, Shade?" she asked suddenly. "Summer in America exemplifies fun. That's not your style."

"It also equals sweat, crops dying from too much sun and frazzled nerves." He lit another cigarette. "More my style?"

"You said it, I didn't." She swirled the chocolate in her mouth. "You smoke like that, you're going to die."

"Sooner or later." Shade opened the paper again and ended the conversation.

Who the hell was he? Bryan asked herself as she leveled the speed at sixty. What factors in his life had brought out the cynicism as well as the genius? There was humor in him—she'd seen it once or twice. But he seemed to allow himself only a certain degree and no more.

Passion? She could attest first-hand that there was a powder keg inside him. What might set it off? If she was certain of one thing about Shade Colby it was that he held himself in rigid control. The passion, the power, the fury—whatever label you gave it—escaped into his work, but not, she was certain, into his personal life. Not often, in any case.

She knew she should be careful and distant; it would be the smartest way to come out of this long-term assignment without scars. Yet she wanted to dig into his character, and she knew she'd have to give in to the temptation. She'd have to press the buttons and watch the results, probably because she didn't like him and was attracted to him at the same time.

She'd told him the truth when she'd said that she couldn't think of anyone else she didn't like. It went hand in hand with her approach to her art—she looked into a person and found qualities, not all of them admirable, not all of them likable, but something, always something that she could understand. She needed to do that with Shade, for herself. And because, though she'd bide her time telling him, she wanted very badly to photograph him.

"Shade, I want to ask you something else."

He didn't glance up from the paper. "Hmm?"

"What's your favorite movie?"

Half annoyed at the interruption, half puzzled at the question, he looked up and found himself wondering yet again what her hair would look like out of that thick, untidy braid. "What?"

"Your favorite movie," she repeated. "I need a clue, a starting point."

"For what?"

"To find out why I find you interesting, attractive and unlikable."

"You're an odd woman, Bryan."

"No, not really, though I have every right to be." She stopped speaking a moment as she switched lanes. "Come on, Shade, it's going to be a long trip. Let's humor each other on the small points. Give me a movie."

"*To Have and Have Not.*"

"Bogart and Bacall's first together." It made her smile at him in the way he'd already decided was dangerous. "Good. If you'd named some obscure French film, I'd have had to find something else. Why that one?"

He set the paper aside. So she wanted to play games. It was harmless, he decided. And they still had a long day ahead of them. "On-screen chemistry, tight plotting and camera work that made Bogart look like the consummate hero and Bacall the only woman who could stand up to him."

She nodded, pleased. He wasn't above enjoying heroes, fantasies and bubbling relationships. It might've been a small point, but she could like him for it. "Movies fascinate me, and the people who make them. I suppose that was one of the reasons I jumped at the chance to work for *Celebrity*. I've lost count of the number of actors I've shot, but when I see them up on the screen, I'm still fascinated."

He knew it was dangerous to ask questions, not because of the answers, but the questions you'd be asked in return. Still, he wanted to know. "Is that why you photograph the beautiful people? Because you want to get close to the glamour?"

Because she considered it a fair question, Bryan decided not to be annoyed. Besides, it made her think about something that had simply seemed to evolve almost unplanned. "I might've started out with something like that in mind. Before long, you come to see them as ordinary people with extraordinary jobs. I like finding that spark that's made them the chosen few."

"Yet for the next three months you're going to be photographing the everyday. Why?"

"Because there's a spark in all of us. I'd like to find it in a farmer in Iowa, too."

So he had his answer. "You're an idealist, Bryan."

"Yes." She gave him a frankly interested look. "Should I be ashamed of it?"

He didn't like the way the calm, reasonable question affected him. He'd had ideals of his own once, and he knew how much it hurt to have them rudely taken away. "Not ashamed," he said after a moment. "Careful."

They drove for hours. In midafternoon, they switched positions and Bryan skimmed through Shade's discarded paper. By mutual consent they left the freeway and began to travel over back roads. The pattern became sporadic conversations and long silences. It was early evening when they crossed the border into Idaho.

"Skiing and potatoes," Bryan commented. "That's all I can think of when I think of Idaho." With a shiver, she rolled up her window. Summer came slower in the north, especially when the sun was low. She gazed out the glass at the deepening twilight.

Sheep, hundreds of them, in what seemed like miles of gray or white bundles were grazing lazily on the tough grass that bordered the road. She was a woman of the city, of freeways and office buildings. It might've surprised Shade to know she'd never been this far north, nor this far east except by plane.

The acres of placid sheep fascinated her. She was reaching for her camera when Shade swore and hit the brakes. Bryan landed on the floor with a plop.

"What was that for?"

He saw at a glance that she wasn't hurt, not even annoyed, but simply curious. He didn't bother to apologize. "Damn sheep in the road."

Bryan hauled herself up and looked out the windshield. There were three of them lined unconcernedly across the road, nearly head to tail. One of them turned its head and glanced up at the van, then looked away again.

"They look like they're waiting for a bus," she decided, then grabbed Shade's wrist before he could lean on the horn. "No, wait a minute. I've never touched one."

Before Shade could comment, she was out of the van and walking toward them. One of them shied a few inches away as she approached, but for the most part, the sheep couldn't have cared less. Shade's annoyance began to fade as she leaned over and touched one. He thought another woman might look the same as she stroked a sable at a furrier. Pleased, tentative and oddly sexual. And the light was good. Taking his camera, he selected a filter.

"How do they feel?"

"Soft—not as soft as I'd thought. Alive. Nothing like a lamb's-wool coat." Still bent over, one hand on the sheep, Bryan looked up. It surprised her to be facing a camera. "What's that for?"

"Discovery." He'd already taken two shots but wanted more. "Discovery has a lot to do with summer. How do they smell?"

Intrigued, Bryan leaned closer to the sheep. He framed her when her face was all but buried in the wool. "Like sheep," she said with a laugh and straightened. "Want to play with the sheep and I'll take your picture?"

"Maybe next time."

She looked as if she belonged there, on the long deserted road surrounded by stretches of empty land, and it puzzled him. He'd thought she set well in L.A., in the center of the glitz and illusions.

"Something wrong?" She knew he was thinking of her, only of her, when he looked at her like that. She wished she could've taken it a step further, yet was oddly relieved that she couldn't.

"You acclimate well."

Her smile was hesitant. "It's simpler that way. I told you I don't like complications."

He turned back to the truck, deciding he was thinking about her too much. "Let's see if we can get these sheep to move."

"But Shade, you can't just leave them on the side of the road." She jogged back to the van. "They'll wander right back out. They might get run over."

He gave her a look that said he clearly wasn't interested. "What do you expect me to do? Round 'em up?"

"The least we can do is get them back over the fence." As if he'd agreed wholeheartedly, Bryan turned around and started back to the sheep. As he watched, she reached down, hauled one up and nearly toppled over. The other two bleated and scattered.

"Heavier than they look," she managed and began to stagger toward the fence strung along the shoulder of the road while the sheep she carried bleated, kicked and struggled. It wasn't easy, but after a test of wills and brute strength, she dropped the sheep over the fence. With one hand she swiped at the sweat on her forehead as she turned to scowl at Shade. "Well, are you going to help or not?"

He'd enjoyed the show, but he didn't smile as he leaned against the van. "They'll probably find the hole in the fence again and be back on the road in ten minutes."

"Maybe they will," Bryan said between her teeth as she headed for the second sheep. "But I'll have done what should be done."

"Idealist," he said again.

With her hands on her hips, she whirled around. "Cynic."

"As long as we understand each other." Shade straightened. "I'll give you a hand."

The others weren't as easily duped as the first. It took Shade several exhausting minutes to catch number two with Bryan running herd. Twice he lost his concentration and his quarry because her sudden husky laughter distracted him.

"Two down and one to go," he announced as he set the sheep free in pasture.

"But this one looks stubborn." From opposite sides of the road, the rescuers and the rescuee studied each other. "Shifty eyes," Bryan murmured. "I think he's the leader."

"She."

"Whatever. Look, just be nonchalant. You walk around that side, I'll walk around this side. When we have her in the middle, wham!"

Shade sent her a cautious look. "Wham?"

"Just follow my lead." Tucking her thumbs in her back pockets, she strolled across the road, whistling.

"Bryan, you're trying to out-think a sheep."

She sent him a bland look over her shoulder. "Maybe between the two of us we can manage to."

He wasn't at all sure she was joking. His first urge was to simply get back in the van and wait until she'd finished making a fool of herself. Then again, they'd already wasted enough time. Shade circled around to the left as Bryan moved to the right. The sheep eyed them both, swiveling her head from side to side.

"Now!" Bryan shouted, and dived.

Without giving himself the chance to consider the absurdity, Shade lunged from the other side. The sheep danced delicately away. Momentum carrying them both, Shade and Bryan collided, then rolled together onto the soft shoulder of the road. Shade felt the rush of air as they slammed into each other, and the soft give of her body as they tumbled together.

With the breath knocked out of her, Bryan lay on her back, half under Shade. His body was very hard and very male. She might not have had her wind, but Bryan had her wit. She knew if they stayed like this, things were going to get complicated. Drawing in air, she stared up into his face just above her.

His look was contemplative, considering and not altogether friendly. He wouldn't be a friendly lover, that she knew instinctively. It was in his eyes—those dark, deep-set eyes. He was definitely a man to avoid having a personal involvement with. He'd overwhelm quickly, completely, and there'd be no turning back. She had to remind herself that she preferred easy relationships, as her heart started a strong steady rhythm.

"Missed," she managed to say, but didn't try to move away.

"Yeah." She had a stunning face, all sharp angles and soft skin. Shade could nearly convince himself that his interest in it was purely professional. She'd photograph wonderfully from any angle, in any light. He could make her look like a queen or a peasant, but she'd always look like a woman a man would want. The lazy sexuality he could sense in her would come across in the photograph.

Just looking at her he could plot half a dozen settings he'd like to shoot her in. And he could think of dozens of ways he'd like to make love to her. Here was first, on the cool grass along the roadside with the sun setting behind them and no sound.

She saw the decision in his eyes, saw it in time to avoid the outcome. But she didn't. She had only to shift away, only to protest with one word or a negative movement. But she didn't. Her mind told her to, arguing with an urge that was unarguably physical. Later, Bryan would wonder why she hadn't listened. Now with the air growing cool and the sky darkening, she wanted the experience. She couldn't admit that she wanted him.

When he lowered his mouth to hers, there wasn't any of the light experimentation of the first time. Now he knew her and wanted the full impact of her passion. Their mouths met greedily, as if each one were racing the other to delirium.

Her body heated so quickly that the grass seemed to shimmer like ice beneath her. She wondered it didn't melt. It was a jolt that left her bewildered. With a small sound in her throat, Bryan reached for more. His fingers were in her hair, tangled in the restriction of her braid as if he didn't choose, or didn't dare, to touch her yet. She moved under him, not in retreat but in advance. Hold me, she seemed to demand. Give me more. But he continued to make love only to her mouth. Devastatingly.

She could hear the breeze; it tickled through the grass beside her ear and taunted her. He'd give sparingly of himself. She could feel it in the tenseness of his body. He'd hold back. While his mouth stripped away her defenses one by one, he held himself apart. Frustrated, Bryan ran her hands up his back. She'd seduce.

Shade wasn't used to the pressure to give, to the desire to. She drew from him a need for merging he'd thought he'd beaten down years before. There seemed to be no pretenses in her—her mouth was warm and eager, tasting of generosity. Her body was soft and agile, tempting. Her scent drifted around him, sexual, uncomplicated. When she said his name, there seemed to be no hidden meaning. For the first time in too long for him to remember, he wanted to give, unheedingly, boundlessly.

He held himself back. Pretenses, he knew, could be well hidden. But he was losing to her. Even though Shade was fully aware of it, he couldn't stop it. She drew and drew from him with a simplicity that couldn't be blocked. He might've sworn against it, cursed her, cursed himself, but his mind was beginning to swim. His body was throbbing.

They both felt the ground tremble, but it didn't occur to either of them that it was anything but their own passion. They heard the noise, the rumble, growing louder and louder, and each thought it was inside his or her own head. Then the wind rocketed by them and the truck driver gave one long, rude blast of the horn. It was enough to jolt them back to sanity. Feeling real panic for the first time, Bryan scrambled to her feet.

"We'd better take care of that sheep and get going." She swore at the breathiness of her own voice and wrapped her arms protectively around herself. There was a chill in the air, she thought desperately. That was all. "It's nearly dark."

Shade hadn't realized how deep the twilight had become. He'd lost track of his surroundings—something he never allowed to happen. He'd forgotten that they were on the side of the road, rolling in the grass like a couple of brainless teenagers. He felt the lick of anger, but stemmed it. He'd nearly lost control once. He wouldn't lose it now.

She caught the sheep on the other side of the road, where it grazed, certain that both humans had lost interest. It bleated in surprised protest as she scooped it up. Swearing under his breath, Shade stalked over and grabbed the sheep from her before Bryan could take another tumble. He dumped it unceremoniously into pasture.

"Satisfied now?" he demanded.

She could see the anger in him, no matter how tightly he reined it in. Her own bubbled. She'd had her share of frustrations as well. Her body was pulsing, her legs unsteady. Temper helped her to forget them.

"No," she tossed back. "And neither are you. It seems to me that should prove to both of us that we'd better keep a nice, clean distance."

He grabbed her arm as she started to swing past. "I didn't force you into anything, Bryan."

"Nor I you," she reminded him. "I'm responsible for my own actions, Shade." She glanced down at the hand that was curled around her arm. "And my own mistakes. If you like to shift blame, it's your prerogative."

His fingers tightened on her arm, briefly, but long enough for her eyes to widen in surprise at the strength and the depth of his anger. No, she wasn't used to wild swings of mood in herself or causing them in others.

Slowly, and with obvious effort, Shade loosened his grip. She'd hit it right on the mark. He couldn't argue with honesty.

"No," he said a great deal more calmly. "I'll take my share, Bryan. It'll be easier on both of us if we agree to that nice, clean distance."

She nodded, steadier. Her lips curved into a slight smile. "Okay." Lighten up, she warned herself, for everyone's sake. "It'd been easier from the beginning if you'd been fat and ugly."

He'd grinned before he'd realized it. "You too."

"Well, since I don't suppose either of us is willing to do anything about that particular problem, we just have to work around it. Agreed?" She held out her hand.

"Agreed."

Their hands joined. A mistake. Neither of them had recovered from the jolt to their systems. The contact, however casual, only served to accentuate it. Bryan linked her hands behind her back. Shade dipped his into his pockets.

"Well . . ." Bryan began, with no idea where to go.

"Let's find a diner before we head into camp. Tomorrow's going to start early."

She wrinkled her nose at that but started toward her side of the truck. "I'm starving," she announced and pretended she was in control by propping her feet on the dash. "Think we'll find something decent to eat soon, or should I fortify myself with a candy bar?"

"There's a town about ten miles down this road." Shade turned on the ignition. His hand was steady, he told himself. Or nearly. "Bound to be a restaurant of some kind. Probably serve great lamb chops."

Bryan looked at the sheep grazing beside them, then sent Shade a narrowed-eyed glance. "That's disgusting."

"Yeah, and it'll keep your mind off your stomach until we eat."

They bumped back onto the road and drove in silence. They'd made it over a hump, but each of them knew there'd be mountains yet to struggle over. Steep, rocky mountains.

Chapter Four

Bryan recorded vacationers floating like corks in the Great Salt Lake. When the shot called for it, she used a long or a wide angle lens to bring in some unusual part of the landscape. But for the most part, Bryan concentrated on the people.

In the salt flats to the west, Shade framed race car enthusiasts. He angled for the speed, the dust, the grit. More often than not, the people included in his pictures would be anonymous, blurred, shadowy. He wanted only the essence.

Trips to large cities and through tidy suburbs used up rolls of film. There were summer gardens, hot, sweaty traffic jams, young girls in thin dresses, shirtless men, and babies in strollers being pushed along sidewalks and in shopping malls.

Their route through Idaho and Utah had been winding, but steady. Neither was displeased with the pace or the subjects. For a time, after the turbulent detour on the country road in Idaho, Bryan and Shade worked side by side in relative harmony. They concentrated on their own subjects, but they did little as a team.

They'd already taken hundreds of pictures, a fraction of which would be printed and still a smaller fraction published. Once it occurred to Bryan that the pictures they'd taken far outnumbered the words they'd spoken to each other.

They drove together up to eight hours a day, stopping along the way whenever it was necessary or desirable to work. And they worked as much as they drove. Out of each twenty-four hours, they were together an average of twenty. But they grew no closer. It was something either of them might have accomplished with the ease of a friendly gesture or a few casual words. It was something both of them avoided.

Bryan learned it was possible to keep an almost obsessive emotional distance from someone while sharing a limited space. She also learned a limited space made it very difficult to ignore what Shade had once termed chemistry. To balance the two, Bryan kept her conversations light and brief and almost exclusively centered on the assignment. She asked no more questions. Shade volunteered no more information.

By the time they crossed the border into Arizona at the end of the first week, she was already finding it an uncomfortable way to work.

It was hot. The sun was merciless. The van's airconditioning helped, but just looking out at the endless desert and faded sage made the mouth dry. Bryan had an enormous paper cup filled with soda and ice. Shade drank bottled iced tea as he drove.

She estimated that they hadn't exchanged a word for fifty-seven miles. Nor had they spoken much that morning when they'd set up to shoot, each in separate territory, at Glen Canyon in Utah. Bryan might be pleased with the study she'd done on the cars lined up at the park's entrance, but she was growing weary of their unspoken agreement of segregation.

The magazine had hired them as a team, she reminded herself. Each of them would take individual pictures, naturally, but there had to be some communication if the photo essay were to have any cohesion. There had to be some blending if the final result was the success both of them wanted. Compromise, she remembered with a sigh. They'd forgotten the operative word.

Bryan thought she knew Shade well enough at this point to be certain he'd never make the first move. He was perfectly capable of driving thousands of miles around the country without saying her name more than once a day. As in, 'pass the salt,' Bryan.

She could be stubborn. Bryan thought about it as she brooded out the window at the wide stretches of Arizona. She could be just as aloof as he. And, she admitted with a grimace, she could bore herself to death within another twenty-four hours.

Contact, she decided. She simply couldn't survive without some kind of contact. Even if it was with a hard-edged, casually rude cynic. Her only choice was to swallow her pride and make the first move herself. She gritted her teeth, gnawed on ice and thought about it for another ten minutes.

"Ever been to Arizona?"

Shade tossed his empty bottle into the plastic can they used for trash. "No."

Bryan pried off one sneaker with the toe of the other. If at first you don't succeed, she told herself. "They filmed *Outcast* in Sedona. Now that was a tough, thinking-man's Western," she mused and received no response. "I spent three days there covering the filming for *Celebrity*." After adjusting her sun visor, she sat back again. "I was lucky enough to miss my plane and get another day. I spent it in Oak Creek Canyon. I've never forgotten it—the colors, the rock formations."

It was the longest speech she'd made in days. Shade negotiated the van around a curve and waited for the rest.

Okay, she thought, she'd get more than one word out of him if she had to use a crowbar. "A friend of mine settled there. Lee used to work for *Celebrity*. Now she's a novelist with her first book due out in the fall. She married Hunter Brown last year."

"The writer?"

Two words, she thought, smug. "Yes, have you read his stuff?"

This time Shade merely nodded and pulled a cigarette out of his pocket. Bryan began to sympathize with dentists who had to coax a patient to open wide.

"I've read everything he's written, then I hate myself for letting his books give me nightmares."

"Good horror fiction's supposed to make you wake up at 3:00 A.M. and wonder if you've locked your doors."

This time she grinned. "That sounds like something Hunter would say. You'll like him."

Shade merely moved his shoulders. He'd agreed to the stop in Sedona already, but he wasn't interested in taking flattering, commercial pictures of the occult king and his family. It would, however, give Shade the break he needed. If he could dump Bryan off for a day or two with her friends, he could take the time to get his system back to normal.

He hadn't had an easy moment since the day they'd started out of L.A. Every day that went by only tightened his nerves and played havoc with his libido. He'd tried, but it wasn't possible to forget she was there within arm's reach at night, separated from him only by the width of the van and the dark.

Yes, he could use a day away from her, and that natural, easy sexuality she didn't even seem aware of.

"You haven't seen them for a while?" he asked her.

"Not in months." Bryan relaxed, more at ease now that they'd actually begun a two-way conversation. "Lee's a good friend. I've missed her. She'll have a baby about the same time her book comes out."

The change in her voice had him glancing over. There was something softer about her now. Almost wistful.

"A year ago, we were both still with *Celebrity*, and now..." She turned to him but the shaded glasses hid her eyes. "It's odd thinking of Lee settled down with a family. She was always more ambitious than me. It used to drive her crazy that I took everything with such a lack of intensity."

"Do you?"

"Just about everything," she murmured. Not you, she thought to herself. I don't seem to be able to take you easily. "It's simpler to relax and live," she went on, "than to worry about how you'll be living next month."

"Some people have to worry *if* they'll be living next month."

"Do you think the fact they worry about it changes things?" Bryan forgot her plan to make contact, forgot the fact that she'd been groping for some sort of compromise from him. He'd seen more than she'd seen of the world, of life. She had to admit that he'd seen more than she wanted to see. But how did he feel about it?

"Being aware can change things. Looking out for yourself's a priority some of us haven't a choice about."

Some of us. She noted the phrase but decided not to pounce on it. If he had scars, he was entitled to keep them covered until they'd faded a bit more.

"Everyone worries from time to time," she decided. 'I'm just not very good at it. I suppose it comes from my parents. They're..." She trailed off and laughed. It occurred to him he hadn't heard her laugh in days, and that

he'd missed it. "I guess they're what's termed bohemi-
ans. We lived in this little house in Carmel that was always in varying states of disrepair. My father would get
a notion to take out a wall or put in a window, then in the
middle of the project, he'd get an inspiration, go back to
his canvases and leave the mess where it lay."

She settled back, no longer aware that she was doing
all the talking and Shade all the listening. "My mother
liked to cook. Trouble was, you'd never know what
mood she'd be in. You might have grilled rattlesnake one
day, cheeseburgers the next. Then when you least expected it, there'd be goose neck stew."

"Goose neck stew?"

"I ate at the neighbors' a lot." The memory brought
on her appetite. Taking out two candy bars, she offered
one to Shade. "How about your parents?"

He unwrapped the candy absently while he paced his
speed to the state police car in the next lane. "They re-
tired to Florida. My father fishes and my mother runs a
craft shop. Not as colorful as yours, I'm afraid."

"Colorful." She thought about it and approved. "I
never knew they were unusual until I'd gone away to
college and realized that most kids' parents were grown
up and sensible. I guess I never realized how much I'd
been influenced by them until Rob pointed out things like
most people preferring to eat dinner at six rather than
scrounging for popcorn or peanut butter at ten o'clock at
night."

"Rob?"

She glanced over quickly, then straight ahead. Shade
listened too well, she decided. It made it too easy to say
more than you intended. "My ex-husband." She knew
she shouldn't still see the "ex" as a stigma; these days it
was nearly a status symbol. For Bryan it was the symbol

that proved she hadn't done what was necessary to keep a promise.

"Still sore?" He'd asked before he could stop himself. She made him want to offer comfort when he'd schooled himself not to become involved in anyone's life, anyone's problem.

"No, it was years ago." After a quick shrug she nibbled on her candy bar. Sore? she thought again. No, not sore, but perhaps she'd always be just a little tender. "Just sorry it didn't work out, I suppose."

"Regrets are more a waste of time than worrying."

"Maybe. You were married once, too."

"That's right." His tone couldn't have been more dismissive. Bryan gave him a long, steady look.

"Sacred territory?"

"I don't believe in rehashing the past."

This wound was covered with scar tissue, she mused. She wondered if it troubled him much or if he'd truly filed it away. In either case, it wasn't her business, nor was it the way to keep the ball rolling between them.

"When did you decide to become a photographer?" That was a safe topic, she reflected. There shouldn't be any tender points.

"When I was five and got my hands on my father's new 35 millimeter. When he had the film developed he discovered three close-ups of the family dog. I'm told he didn't know whether to congratulate me or give me solitary confinement when they turned out to be better than any of his shots."

Bryan grinned. "What'd he do?"

"He bought me a camera of my own."

"You were way ahead of me," she commented. "I didn't have any interest in cameras until high school. Just sort of fell into it. Up until then, I'd wanted to be a star."

"An actress?"

"No." She grinned again. "A star. Any kind of a star as long as I had a Rolls, a gold lamé dress and a big tacky diamond."

He had to grin. She seemed to have the talent for forcing it out of him. "An unassuming child."

"No, materialistic." She offered him her drink but he shook his head. "That stage coincided with my parents' return-to-the-earth period. I guess it was my way of rebelling against people who were almost impossible to rebel against."

He glanced down at her ringless hands and her faded jeans. "Guess you got over it."

"I wasn't made to be a star. Anyway, they needed someone to take pictures of the football team." Bryan finished off the candy bar and wondered how soon they could stop for lunch. "I volunteered because I had a crush on one of the players." Draining her soda, she dumped the cup in with Shade's bottle. "After the first day I fell in love with the camera and forgot all about the defensive lineman."

"His loss."

Bryan glanced over, surprised by the offhand compliment. "That was a nice thing to say, Colby. I didn't think you had it in you."

He didn't quite defeat the smile. "Don't get used to it."

"Heaven forbid." But she was a great deal more pleased than his casual words warranted. "Anyway, my parents were thrilled when I became an obsessive photographer. They'd lived with this deadly fear that I had no creative drives and would end up being a smashing business success instead of an artist."

"So now you're both."

She thought about it a moment. Odd how easy it was to forget about one aspect of her work when she concentrated so hard on the other. "I suppose you're right. Just don't mention it to Mom and Dad."

"They won't hear it from me."

They both saw the construction sign at the same time. Whether either of them realized it, their minds followed the same path. Bryan was already reaching for her camera when Shade slowed and eased off the road. Ahead of them a road crew patched, graded and sweat under the high Arizona sun.

Shade walked off to consider the angle that would show the team and machinery battling against the erosion of the road. A battle that would be waged on roads across the country each summer as long as roads existed. Bryan homed in on one man.

He was bald and had a yellow bandanna tied around his head to protect the vulnerable dome of his scalp. His face and neck were reddened and damp, his belly sagging over the belt of his work pants. He wore a plain white T-shirt, pristine compared to the colorful ones slashed with sayings and pictures the workmen around him chose.

To get in close she had to talk to him and deal with the comments and grins from the rest of the crew. She did so with an aplomb and charm that would've caused a public relations expert to rub his hands together. Bryan was a firm believer that the relationship between the photographer and the subject showed through in the final print. So first, in her own way, she had to develop one.

Shade kept his distance. He saw the men as a team—the sunburned, faceless team that worked roads across the country and had done so for decades. He wanted no relationship with any of them, nothing that would color the way he saw them as they stood, bent and dug.

He took a telling shot of the grime, dust and sweat. Bryan learned that the foreman's name was Al and he'd worked for the road commission for twenty-two years.

It took her a while to ease her way around his self-consciousness, but once she got him talking about what the miserable winter had done to his road, everything clicked. Sweat dribbled down his temple. When he reached up with one beefy arm to swipe at it, Bryan had her picture.

The impulsive detour took them thirty minutes. By the time they piled back in the van, they were sweating as freely as the laborers.

"Are you always so personal with strangers?" Shade asked her as he switched on the engine and the air-conditioning.

"When I want their picture, sure." Bryan opened the cooler and pulled out one of the cold cans she'd stocked and another bottle of iced tea for Shade. "You get what you wanted?"

"Yeah."

He'd watched her at work. Normally they separated, but this time he'd been close enough to see just how she went about her job. She'd treated the road man with more respect and good humor than many photographers treated their hundred-dollar-an-hour models. And she hadn't done it just for the picture, though Shade wasn't sure she realized it. She'd been interested in the man—who he was, what he was and why.

Once, a long time before, Shade had had that kind of curiosity. Now he strapped it down. Knowing involved you. But it wasn't easy, he was discovering, to strap down his curiosity about Bryan. Already she'd told him more than he'd have asked. Not more than he wanted to know, but more than he'd have asked. It still wasn't enough.

For nearly a week he'd backed off from her—just as far as it was possible under the circumstances. He hadn't stopped wanting her. He might not like to rehash the past, but it wasn't possible to forget that last molten encounter on the roadside.

He'd closed himself off, but now she was opening him up again. He wondered if it was foolish to try to fight it, and the attraction they had for each other. It might be better, simpler, more logical to just let things progress to the only possible conclusion.

They'd sleep together, burn the passion out and get back to the assignment.

Cold? Calculated? Perhaps, but he'd do nothing except follow the already routed course. He knew it was important to keep the emotions cool and the mind sharp.

He'd let his emotions fuddle his logic and his perception before. In Cambodia a sweet face and a generous smile had blinded him to treachery. Shade's fingers tightened on the wheel without his realizing it. He'd learned a lesson about trust then—it was only the flip side of betrayal.

"Where've you gone?" Bryan asked quietly. A look had come into his eyes she didn't understand, and wasn't certain she wanted to.

He turned his head. For an instant she was caught in the turmoil, in the dark place he remembered too well and she knew nothing about. Then it was over. His eyes were remote and calm. His fingers eased on the wheel.

"We'll stop in Page," he said briefly. "Get some shots of the boats and tourists on Lake Powell before we go down to the canyon."

"All right."

He hadn't been thinking of her. Bryan could comfort herself with that. She hoped the look that had come into his eyes would never be applied to her. Even so, she was determined that sooner or later she'd discover the reason for it.

She could've gotten some good technical shots of the dam. But as they passed through the tiny town of Page, heading for the lake, Bryan saw the high golden arches shimmering behind waves of heat. It made her grin. Cheeseburgers and fries weren't just summer pastimes. They'd become a way of life. Food for all seasons. But she couldn't resist the sight of the familiar building settled low below the town, almost isolated like a mirage in the middle of the desert.

She rolled down her window and waited for the right angle. "Gotta eat," she said as she framed the building. "Just gotta." She clicked the shutter.

Resigned, Shade pulled into the lot. "Get it to go," he ordered as Bryan started to hop out. "I want to get to the marina."

Swinging her purse over her shoulder, she disappeared inside. Shade didn't have the chance to become impatient before she bounded back out again with two white bags. "Cheap, fast and wonderful," she told him as she slid back into her seat. "I don't know how I'd make it through life if I couldn't get a cheeseburger on demand."

She pulled out a wrapped burger and handed it to him.

"I got extra salt," she said over her first taste of fries. "Mmm, I'm starving."

"You wouldn't be if you'd eat something besides a candy bar for breakfast."

"I'd rather be awake when I eat," she mumbled, involved in unwrapping her burger.

Shade unwrapped his own. He hadn't asked her to bring him anything. He'd already learned it was typical of her to be carelessly considerate. Perhaps the better word was naturally. But it wasn't typical of him to be moved by the simple offer of a piece of meat in a bun. He reached in a bag and brought out a paper napkin. "You're going to need this."

Bryan grinned, took it, folded her legs under her and dug in. Amused, Shade drove leisurely to the marina.

They rented a boat, what Bryan termed a putt-putt. It was narrow, open and about the size of a canoe. It would, however, carry them, and what equipment they chose, out on the lake.

She liked the little marina with its food stands and general stores with displays of suntan oil and bathing suits. The season was in full swing; people strolled by dressed in shorts and cover-ups, in hats and sunglasses. She spotted a teenage couple, brown and gleaming, on a bench, licking at dripping ice-cream cones. Because they were so involved with each other, Bryan was able to take some candid shots before the paperwork on the rental was completed.

Ice cream and suntans. It was a simple, cheerful way to look at summer. Satisfied, she secured her camera in its bag and went back to Shade.

"Do you know how to drive a boat?"

He sent her a mild look as they walked down the dock. "I'll manage."

A woman in a neat white shirt and shorts gave them a rundown, pointing out the life jackets and explaining the engine before she handed them a glossy map of the lake.

Bryan settled herself in the bow and prepared to enjoy herself.

"The nice thing about this," she called over the engine, "is it's so unexpected." She swept one arm out to indicate the wide expanse of blue.

Red-hued mesas and sheer rock walls rose up steeply to cradle the lake, settled placidly where man had put it. The combination was fascinating to her. Another time she might've done a study on the harmony and power that could result in a working relationship between human imagination and nature.

It wasn't necessary to know all the technical details of the dam, of the labor force that built it. It was enough that it was, that they were here—cutting through water that had once been desert, sending up a spray that had once been sand.

Shade spotted a tidy cabin cruiser and veered in its direction. For the moment he'd navigate and leave the camera work to Bryan. It'd been a long time since he'd spent a hot afternoon on the water. His muscles began to relax even as his perception sharpened.

Before he was done he'd have to take some pictures of the rocks. The texture in them was incredible, even in their reflection on the water. Their colors, slashed against the blue lake, made them look surreal. He'd make the prints sharp and crisp to accent the incongruity. He edged a bit closer to the cabin cruiser as he planned the shot for later.

Bryan took out her camera without any definite plan. She hoped there'd be a party of people, perhaps greased up against the sun. Children maybe, giddy with the wind and water. As Shade steered, she glanced toward the stern and lifted the camera quickly. It was too good to be true.

Poised at the stern of the cruiser was a hound—Bryan couldn't think of any other description for the floppy dog. His big ears were blowing back, his tongue lolling as he stared down at the water. Over his chestnut fur was a bright orange life vest.

"Go around again," she yelled to Shade.

She waited impatiently for the angle to come to her again. There were people on the boat, at least five of them, but they no longer interested her. Just the dog, she thought, as she gnawed on her lip and waited. She wanted nothing but the dog in the life jacket leaning out and staring down at the water.

There were towering mesas just behind the boat. Bryan had to decide quickly whether to work them in or frame them out. If she'd had more time to think ... She opted against the drama and settled on the fun. Shade had circled the trim little cruiser three times before she was satisfied.

"Wonderful!" With a laugh, Bryan lowered her camera. "That one print's going to be worth the whole trip."

He veered off to the right. "Why don't we see what else we can dig up anyway?"

They worked for two hours, shifting positions after the first. Stripped to the waist as defense against the heat, Shade knelt at the bow and focused in on a tour boat. The rock wall rose in the background, the water shimmered cool and blue. Along the rail the people were no more than a blur of color. That's what he wanted. The anonymity of tours, and the power of what drew the masses to them.

While Shade worked, Bryan kept the speed low and looked at everything. She'd decided after one glimpse of his lean, tanned torso that it'd be wiser for her to concentrate on the scenery. If she hadn't been, she might've missed the cove and the rock island that curved over it.

"Look." Without hesitating, she steered toward it, then cut the engines until the boat drifted in its own wake. "Come on, let's take a swim." Before he could comment, she'd hopped out in the ankle-deep water and was securing the lines with rocks.

Wearing a snug tank top and drawstring shorts, Bryan dashed down to the cove and sank in over her head. When she surfaced, laughing, Shade was standing on the island above her. "Fabulous," she called out. "Come on, Shade, we haven't taken an hour to play since we started."

She was right about that. He'd seen to it. Not that he hadn't needed to relax, but he'd thought it best not to around her. He knew, even as he watched her smoothly treading in the rock-shadowed water, that it was a mistake. Yet he'd told himself it was logical to stop fighting what would happen between them. Following the logic, he walked down to the water.

"It's like opening a present," she decided, shifting onto her back to float briefly. "I had no idea I was being slowly boiled until I stepped in here." With a sigh, she dipped under the water and rose again so that it flowed from her face. "There was a pond a few miles away from home when I was a kid. I practically lived there in the summer."

The water was seductive, almost painfully so. As Shade lowered himself into it he felt the heat drain, but not the tension. Sooner or later, he knew, he'd have to find an outlet for it.

"We did a lot better here than I expected to." Lazily she let the water play through her fingers. "I can't wait to get to Sedona and start developing." She tossed her dripping braid behind her back. "And sleep in a real bed."

"You don't seem to have any trouble sleeping." One of the first things he'd noticed was that she could fall asleep anywhere, anytime and within seconds of shutting her eyes.

"Oh, it's not the sleeping, it's the waking up." And waking up only a few feet away from him, morning after morning—seeing his face shadowed by a night's growth of beard, dangerously attractive, seeing his muscles ripple as he stretched, dangerously strong. No, she couldn't deny that the accommodations occasionally gave her a few twinges.

"You know," she began casually, "the budget could handle a couple of motel rooms every week or so—nothing outrageous. A real mattress and a private shower, you know. Some of those campgrounds we've stopped in advertise hot water with their tongues in their cheeks."

He had to smile. It hadn't given him much pleasure to settle for tepid water after a long day on the road. But there was no reason to make it too easy on her. "Can't handle roughing it, Bryan?"

She stretched out on her back again, deliberately kicking water up and over him. "Oh, I don't mind roughing it," she said blandly. "I just like to do it on my own time. And I'm not ashamed to say I'd rather spend the weekend at the Beverly Wilshire than rubbing two sticks together in the wilderness." She closed her eyes and let her body drift. "Wouldn't you?"

"Yeah." With the admission he reached out, grabbed her braid and tugged her head under.

The move surprised her, but it pleased her as well, even as she came up sputtering. So he was capable of a frivolous move from time to time. It was something else she could like him for.

"I'm an expert on water games," she warned him as she began to tread again.

"Water suits you." When had he relaxed? He couldn't pinpoint the moment when the tension began to ease from him. There was something about her—laziness? No, that wasn't true. She worked every bit as hard as he, though in her own fashion. Easiness was a better word, he decided. She was an easy woman, comfortable with herself and whatever surroundings she found herself in.

"It looks pretty good on you, too." Narrowing her eyes, Bryan focused on him—something she'd avoided for several days. If she didn't allow herself a clear look it helped bank down on the feelings he brought out in her. Many of them weren't comfortable, and Shade had been right. She was a woman who liked to be comfortable. But now, with the water lapping cool around her and the only sound that of boats putting in the distance, she wanted to enjoy him.

His hair was damp and tangled around his face, which was as relaxed as she'd ever seen it. There didn't seem to be any secrets in his eyes just now. He was nearly too lean, but there were muscles in his forearms, in his back. She already knew just how strong his hands were. She smiled at him because she wasn't sure just how many quiet moments they'd share.

"You don't let up on yourself enough, Shade."

"No?"

"No. You know..." She floated again because treading took too much effort. "I think deep down, really deep down, there's a nice person in you."

"No, there isn't."

But she heard the humor in his voice. "Oh, it's buried in there somewhere. If you let me do your portrait, I'd find it."

He liked the way she floated in the water; there was absolutely no energy expended. She lay there, trusting buoyancy. He was nearly certain that if she lay quietly for five minutes, she'd be asleep. "Would you?" he murmured. "I think we can both do without that."

She opened her eyes again, but had to squint against the sun to see him. It was at his back, glaring. "Maybe you can, but I've already decided to do it—once I know you better."

He circled her ankle with his finger, lightly. "You have to have my cooperation to do both."

"I'll get it." The contact was more potent than she could handle. She'd tensed before she could stop it. And so, she realized after a long ten seconds, had he. Casually, she let her legs drop. "The water's getting cold." She swam toward the boat with smooth strokes and a racing heart.

Shade waited a moment. No matter what direction he took with her, he always ended up in the same place. He wanted her, but wasn't certain he could handle the consequences of acting on that desire. Worse now, she was perilously close to becoming his friend. That wouldn't make things any easier on either of them.

Slowly, he swam out of the cove and toward the boat, but she wasn't there. Puzzled, he looked around and started to call, when he saw her perched high on the rock.

She'd unbraided her hair and was brushing it dry in the sun. Her legs were folded under her, her face tilted up. The thin summer clothes she wore were drenched and clung to every curve. She obviously didn't care. It was the sun she sought, the heat, just as she'd sought the cool water only moments before.

Shade reached in his camera bag and attached his long lens. He wanted her to fill the viewfinder. He focused and framed her. For the second time her careless sexuality gave him a staggering roundhouse punch. He was a professional, Shade reminded himself as he set the depth of field. He was shooting a subject, that was all.

But when she turned her head and her eyes met his through the lens, he felt the passion sizzle—from himself and from her. They held each other there a moment, separated, yet irrevocably joined. He took the picture, and as he did, Shade knew he was recording a great deal more than a subject.

A bit steadier, Bryan rose and worked her way down the curve of the rock. She had to remind herself to play it lightly—something that had always come easily to her. "You didn't get a release form, Colby," she reminded him as she dropped her brush into her oversize bag.

Reaching out, he touched her hair. It was damp, hanging rich and heavy to her waist. His fingers curled into it, his eyes locked on hers. "I want you."

She felt her legs liquefy, and heat started somewhere in the pit of her stomach and spread out to her fingertips. He was a hard man, Bryan reminded herself. He wouldn't give, but take. In the end, she'd need him to do both.

"That's not good enough for me," she said steadily. "People want all the time—a new car, a color TV. I have to have more than that."

She stepped around him and into the boat. Without a word, Shade joined her and they drifted away from the cove. As the boat picked up speed, both of them wondered if Shade could give any more than what he'd offered.

Chapter Five

Bryan had romanticized Oak Creek Canyon over the years since she'd been there. When she saw it again, she wasn't disappointed. It had all the rich strength, all the colors she'd remembered.

Campers would be pocketed through it, she knew. They'd be worth some time and some film. Amateur and serious fishermen by the creek, she mused, with their intense expressions and colorful lures. Evening campfires with roasting marshmallows. Coffee in tin cups. Yes, it would be well worth the stop.

They planned to stay for three days, working, developing and printing. Bryan was itching to begin. But before they drove into town to handle the details, they'd agreed to stop in the canyon where Bryan could see Lee and her family.

"According to the directions, there should be a little dirt road leading off to the right just beyond a trading post."

Shade watched for it. He, too, was anxious to begin. Some of the shots he'd taken were pulling at him to bring them to life. He needed the concentration and quiet of the darkroom, the solitude of it. He needed to let his creativity flow, and hold in his hands the results.

The picture of Bryan sitting on the island of rock. He didn't like to dwell on that one, but he knew it would be the first roll he developed.

The important thing was that he'd have the time and the distance he'd promised himself. Once he dropped her at her friends'—and he was certain they'd want her to stay with them—he could go into Sedona, rent the darkroom and a motel room for himself. After living with her for twenty-four hours a day, he was counting on a few days apart to steady his system.

They'd each work on whatever they chose—the town, the canyon, the landscape. That gave him room. He'd work out a schedule for the darkroom. With luck, they wouldn't so much as see each other for the next three days.

"There it is," Bryan told him, though he'd already seen the narrow road and slowed for it. She looked at the steep tree-lined road and shook her head. "God, I'd never have pictured Lee here. It's so wild and rough and she's . . . well, elegant."

He'd known a few elegant women in his life. He'd lived with one. Shade glanced at the terrain. "What's she doing here, then?"

"She fell in love," Bryan said simply and leaned forward. "There's the house. Fabulous."

Glass and style. That's what she thought of it. It wasn't the distinguished town house she would have imagined for Lee, but Bryan could see how it would suit her friend. There were flowers blooming, bright red-orange blossoms she couldn't identify. The grass was thick, the trees leafy.

In the driveway were two vehicles, a dusty late-model Jeep and a shiny cream-colored sedan. As they pulled up behind the Jeep, a huge silver-gray form bounded around the side of the house. Shade swore in sheer astonishment.

"That must be Santanas." Bryan laughed but gave the dog a wary going-over with her door firmly closed.

Fascinated, Shade watched the muscles bunch as the dog moved. But the tail was wagging, the tongue lolling. Some pet, he decided. "It looks like a wolf."

"Yeah." She continued to look out the window as the dog paced up and down the side of the van. "Lee tells me he's friendly."

"Fine. You go first."

Bryan shot him a look that he returned with a casual smile. Letting out a deep breath, Bryan opened the door. "Nice dog," she told him as she stepped out, keeping one hand on the handle of the door. "Nice Santanas."

"I read somewhere that Brown raised wolves," Shade said carelessly as he stepped out of the opposite side.

"Cute," Bryan mumbled and cautiously offered her hand for the dog to sniff.

He did so, and obviously liked her because he knocked her to the ground in one bounding leap. Shade was around the van before Bryan had a chance to draw a breath. Fear and fury had carried him, but whatever he might've done was stopped by the sound of a high whistle.

"Santanas!" A young girl darted around the house, braids flying. "Cut it out right now. You're not supposed to knock people down."

Caught in the act, the huge dog plopped down on his belly and somehow managed to look innocent. "He's sorry." The girl looked at the tense man looming over the dog and the breathless woman sprawled beside him. "He just gets excited when company comes. Are you Bryan?"

Bryan managed a nod as the dog dropped his head on her arm and looked up at her.

"It's a funny name. I thought you'd look funny too, but you don't. I'm Sarah."

"Hello, Sarah." Catching her wind, Bryan looked up at Shade. "This is Shade Colby."

"Is that a real name?" Sarah demanded.

"Yeah." Shade looked down as the girl frowned up at him. He wanted to scold her for not handling her dog, but found he couldn't. She had dark, serious eyes that made him want to crouch down and look into them from her level. A heartbreaker, he decided. Give her ten years and she'll break them all.

"Sounds like something from one of my dad's books. I guess it's okay." She grinned down at Bryan and shuffled her sneakers in the dirt. Both she and her dog looked embarrassed. "I'm really sorry Santanas knocked you down. You're not hurt or anything, are you?"

Since it was the first time anyone had bothered to ask, Bryan thought about it. "No."

"Well, maybe you won't say anything to my dad." Sarah flashed a quick smile and showed her braces. "He gets mad when Santanas forgets his manners."

Santanas swiped an enormous pink tongue over Bryan's shoulder.

"No harm done," she decided.

"Great. We'll go tell them you're here." She was off in a bound. The dog clambered up and raced after her without giving Bryan a backward look.

"Well, it doesn't look like Lee's settled for a dull life," Bryan commented.

Shade reached down and hauled her to her feet. He'd been frightened, he realized. Seriously frightened for the first time in years, and all because a little girl's pet had knocked down his partner.

"You okay?"

"Yeah." With quick swipes she began to brush the dirt off her jeans. Shade ran his hands up her arms, stopping her cold.

"Sure?"

"Yes, I...". She trailed off as her thoughts twisted into something incoherent. He wasn't supposed to look at her like that, she thought. As though he really cared. She wished he'd look at her like that again, and again. His fingers were barely touching her arms. She wished he'd touch her like this again. And again.

"I'm fine," she managed finally. But it was hardly more than a whisper, and her eyes never left his.

He kept his hands on her arms. "That dog had to weigh a hundred and twenty."

"He didn't mean any harm." Why, she wondered vaguely, were they talking about a dog when there really wasn't anything important but him and her?

"I'm sorry." His thumb skimmed over the inside of her elbow where the skin was as soft as he'd once imagined. Her pulse beat like an engine. "I should've gotten out first instead of playing around." If she'd been hurt... He wanted to kiss her now, right now, when he was thinking only of her and not the reasons that he shouldn't.

"It doesn't matter," she murmured and found that her hands were resting on his shoulders. Their bodies were close, just brushing. Who had moved? "It doesn't matter," she said again, half to herself as she leaned closer. Their lips hovered, hesitated, then barely touched. From the house came the deep, frantic sound of barking. They drew back from each other with something close to a jerk.

"Bryan!" Lee let the door slam behind her as she came onto the porch. It wasn't until she'd already called out

that she noticed how intent the two people in her driveway were on each other.

With a quick shudder, Bryan took another step back
before she turned. Too many feelings, was all she could
think. Too many feelings too quickly.

"Lee." She ran over—or ran away—she wasn't certain. All she knew was at that moment she needed someone. Grateful, she felt herself closed in Lee's arms. "Oh
God, it's so good to see you."

The greeting was just a little desperate. Lee took a long
look over Bryan's shoulder at the man who remained
several paces back. Her first impression was that he
wanted to stay that way. Separate. What had Bryan gotten herself into? she wondered and gave her friend a
fierce hug.

"I've got to look at you," Bryan insisted, laughing
now as the tension drained. The elegant face, the carefully styled hair—they were the same. But the woman
wasn't. Bryan could feel it before she glanced down to the
rounded swell beneath Lee's crisp summer dress.

"You're happy." Bryan gripped Lee's hands. "It
shows. No regrets?"

"No regrets." Lee took a long, hard study. Bryan
looked the same, she decided. Healthy, easy, lovely in a
way that seemed exclusively her own. The same, she
thought, but for the slightest hint of trouble in her eyes.
"And you?"

"Things are good. I've missed you, but I feel better
about it after seeing you here."

With a laugh, Lee slipped her arm around Bryan's
waist. If there was trouble, she'd find the source. Bryan
was hopeless at hiding anything for long. "Come inside.
Sarah and Hunter are making iced tea." She sent a significant look in Shade's direction and felt Bryan tense.

Just a little, but Lee felt it and knew she'd already found the source.

Bryan cleared her throat. "Shade."

He moved forward, Lee thought, like a man who was used to testing the way.

"Lee Radcliffe—Lee Radcliffe Brown," she corrected and relaxed a bit. "Shade Colby. You remember when I spent the money I'd saved for a new car on one of his prints."

"Yes, I told you you were crazy." Lee extended her hand and smiled, but her voice was cool. "It's nice to meet you. Bryan's always admired your work."

"But you haven't," he returned with more interest and respect than he'd intended to feel.

"I often find it harsh, but always compelling," Lee said simply. "Bryan's the expert, not me."

"Then she'd tell you that we don't take pictures for experts."

Lee nodded. His handshake had been firm—not gentle, but far from cruel. His eyes were precisely the same. She'd have to reserve judgment for now. "Come inside, Mr. Colby."

He'd intended to simply drop Bryan off and move along, but he found himself accepting. It wouldn't hurt, he rationalized, to cool off a bit before he drove into town. He followed the women inside.

"Dad, if you don't put more sugar in it, it tastes terrible."

As they walked into the kitchen, they saw Sarah with her hands on her hips watching her father mop up around a pitcher of tea.

"Not everyone wants to pour sugar into their system the way you do."

"I do." Bryan grinned when Hunter turned. She thought his work brilliant—often cursing him for it in the middle of the night when it kept her awake. She thought he looked like a man one of the Brontë sisters would have written about—strong, dark, brooding. But more, he was the man who loved her closest friend. Bryan opened her arms to him.

"It's good to see you again." Hunter held her close, chuckling when he felt her reach behind him to the plate of cookies Sarah had set out. "Why don't you gain weight?"

"I keep trying," Bryan claimed and bit into the chocolate chip cookie. "Mmm, still warm. Hunter, this is Shade Colby."

Hunter put down his dishcloth. "I've followed your work," he told Shade as they shook hands. "It's powerful."

"That's the word I'd use to describe yours."

"Your latest had me too paranoid to go down to the basement laundry room for weeks," Bryan accused Hunter. "I nearly ran out of clothes."

Hunter grinned, pleased. "Thanks."

She glanced around the sunlit kitchen. "I guess I expected your house to have cobwebs and creaking boards."

"Disappointed?" Lee asked.

"Relieved."

With a laugh, Lee settled at the kitchen table with Sarah on her left and Bryan across from her. "So how's the project going?"

"Good." But Lee noticed she didn't look at Shade as she spoke. "Maybe terrific. We'll know more once we develop the film. We've made arrangements with one of the local papers for the use of a darkroom. All we have to do is drive into Sedona, check in and get a couple of rooms. Tomorrow, we work."

"Rooms?" Lee set down the glass Hunter handed her. "But you're staying here."

"Lee." Bryan gave Hunter a quick smile as he offered the plate of cookies. "I wanted to see you, not drop in bag and baggage. I know both you and Hunter are working on new books. Shade and I'll be up to our ears in developing fluid."

"How are we supposed to visit if you're in Sedona?" Lee countered. "Damn it, Bryan, I've missed you. You're staying here." She laid a hand on her rounded stomach. "Pregnant women have to be pampered."

"You should stay," Shade put in before Bryan could comment. "It might be the last chance for quite a while for a little free time."

"We've a lot of work to do," Bryan reminded him.

"It's a short drive into town from here. That won't make any difference. We're going to need to rent a car, in any case, so we can both be mobile."

Hunter studied the man across the room. Tense, he thought. Intense. Not the sort of man he'd have picked for the free-rolling, slow-moving Bryan, but it wasn't his place to judge. It was his place, and his talent, to observe. What was between them was obvious to see. Their reluctance to accept it was just as obvious. Calmly, he picked up his tea and drank.

"The invitation applies to both of you."

Shade glanced over with an automatic polite refusal on the tip of his tongue. His eyes met Hunter's. They were both intense, internalized men. Perhaps that's why they understood each other so quickly.

I've been there before, Hunter seemed to say to him with a hint of a smile. *You can run fast but only so far.*

Shade sensed something of the understanding, and something of the challenge. He glanced down to see Bryan giving him a long, cool look.

"I'd love to stay," he heard himself say. Shade crossed to the table and sat.

Lee looked over the prints in her precise, deliberate way. Bryan paced up and down the terrace, ready to explode.

"Well?" she demanded. "What do you think?"

"I haven't finished looking through them yet."

Bryan opened her mouth, then shut it again. It wasn't like her to be nervous over her work. She knew the prints were good. Hadn't she put her sweat and her heart into each of them?

More than good, she told herself as she yanked a chocolate bar out of her pocket. These prints ranked with her best work. It might've been the competition with Shade that had pushed her to produce them. It might've been the need to feel a bit smug after some of the comments he'd made on her particular style of work. Bryan didn't like to think she was base enough to resort to petty rivalry, but she had to admit that now she was. And she wanted to win.

She and Shade had lived in the same house, worked in the same darkroom for days, but had managed to see almost nothing of each other. A neat trick, Bryan thought ruefully. Perhaps it had worked so well because they'd both played the same game. Hide and don't seek. Tomorrow they'd be back on the road.

Bryan found that she was anxious to go even while she dreaded it. And she wasn't a contrary person, Bryan reminded herself almost fiercely. She was basically straightforward and...well, yes, she was amiable. It was simply her nature to be. So why wasn't she with Shade?

"Well."

Bryan whirled around as Lee spoke. "Well?" she echoed, waiting.

"I've always admired your work, Bryan. You know that." In her tidy way, Lee folded her hands on the wrought-iron table.

"But?" Bryan prompted.

"But these are the best." Lee smiled. "The very best you've ever done."

Bryan let out the breath she'd been holding and crossed to the table. Nerves? Yes, she had them. She didn't care for them. "Why?"

"I'm sure there're a lot of technical reasons—the light and the shading, the cropping."

Impatiently, Bryan shook her head. "Why?"

Understanding, Lee chose a print. "This one of the old woman and the little girl on the beach. Maybe it's my condition," she said slowly as she studied it again, "but it makes me think of the child I'll have. It also makes me remember I'll grow old, but not too old to dream. This picture's powerful because it's so basically simple, so straightforward and so incredibly full of emotion. And this one..."

She shuffled the prints until she came to the one of the road worker. "Sweat, determination, honesty. You know when you look at this face that the man believes in hard work and paying his bills on time. And here, these teenagers. I see youth just before those inevitable changes of adulthood. And this dog." Lee laughed as she looked at it. "The first time I looked, it just struck me as cute and funny, but he looks so proud, so, well, human. You could almost believe the boat was his."

While Bryan remained silent, Lee tidied the prints again. "I could go over each one of them with you, but the point is, each one of them tells a story. It's only one scene, one instant of time, yet the story's there. The feelings are there. Isn't that the purpose?"

"Yes." Bryan smiled as her shoulders relaxed. "That's the purpose."

"If Shade's pictures are half as good, you'll have a wonderful essay."

"They will be," Bryan murmured. "I saw some of his negatives in the darkroom. They're incredible."

Lee lifted a brow and watched Bryan devour chocolate. "Does that bother you?"

"What? Oh, no, no, of course not. His work is his work—and in this case it'll be part of mine. I'd never have agreed to work with him if I hadn't admired him."

"But?" This time Lee prompted with a raised brow and half smile.

"I don't know, Lee, he's just so—so perfect."

"Really?"

"He never fumbles," Bryan complained. "He always knows exactly what he wants. When he wakes up in the morning, he's perfectly coherent, he never misses a turn on the road. He even makes decent coffee."

"Anyone would detest him for that," Lee said dryly.

"It's frustrating, that's all."

"Love often is. You are in love with him, aren't you?"

"No." Genuinely surprised, Bryan stared over at Lee. "Good God, I hope I've more sense than that. I have to work hard at even liking him."

"Bryan, you're my friend. Otherwise what I'm calling concern would be called prying."

"Which means you're going to pry," Bryan put in.

"Exactly. I've seen the way the two of you tiptoe around each other as if you're terrified that if you happened to brush up against each other there'd be spontaneous combustion."

"Something like that."

Lee reached out and touched her hand. "Bryan, tell me."

Evasions weren't possible. Bryan looked down at the joined hands and sighed. "I'm attracted," she admitted slowly. "He's different from anyone I've known, mostly because he's just not the type of man I'd normally socialize with. He's very remote, very serious. I like to have fun. Just fun."

"Relationships have to be made up of more than just fun."

"I'm not looking for a relationship." On this point she was perfectly clear. "I date so I can go dancing, go to a party, listen to music or see a movie. That's it. The last thing I want is all the tension and work that goes into a relationship."

"If someone didn't know you, they'd say that was a pretty shallow sentiment."

"Maybe it is," Bryan tossed back. "Maybe I am."

Lee said nothing, just tapped a finger on the prints.

"That's my work," Bryan began, then gave up. A lot of people might believe what she said on face value, not Lee. "I don't want a relationship," she repeated, but in a quieter tone. "Lee, I've been there before and I'm lousy at it."

"Relationship equals two," Lee pointed out. "Are you still taking the blame?"

"Most of the blame was mine. I was no good at being a wife."

"At being a certain kind of wife," Lee corrected.

"I imagine there's only a handful of definitions in the dictionary."

Lee only raised a brow. "Sarah has a friend whose mother is wonderful. She keeps not just a clean house, but an interesting one. She makes jelly, takes the minutes at the P.T.A. and runs a Girl Scout troop. The woman can take a colored paper and some glue and create a work of art. She's lovely and helps herself stay that way with exercise classes three times a week. I admire her a great deal, but if Hunter had wanted those things from me, I wouldn't have his ring on my finger."

"Hunter's special," Bryan murmured.

"I can't argue with that. And you know why I nearly ruined it with him—because I was afraid I'd fail at building and maintaining a relationship."

"It's not a matter of being afraid." Bryan shrugged her shoulders. "It's more a matter of not having the energy for it."

"Remember who you're talking to," Lee said mildly.

With a half laugh, Bryan shook her head. "All right, maybe it's a matter of being cautious. Relationship's a very weighty word. Affair's lighter," she said consideringly. "But an affair with a man like Shade's bound to have tremendous repercussions."

That sounded so cool, Bryan mused. When had she started to think in such logical terms? "He's not an easy man, Lee. He has his own demons and his own way of dealing with them. I don't know whether he'd share them with me or if I'd want him to."

"He works at being cold," Lee commented. "But I've seen him with Sarah. I admit the basic kindness in him surprised me, but it's there."

"It's there," Bryan agreed. "It's just hard to get to."

"Dinner's ready!" Sarah yanked open the screen door and let it hit the wall with a bang. "Shade and I made spaghetti and it's terrific."

It was. During the meal, Bryan watched Shade. Like Lee, she'd noticed his easy relationship with Sarah. It was more than tolerance, she decided as she watched him laugh with the girl. It was affection. It hadn't occurred to her that Shade could give his affection so quickly or with so few restrictions.

Maybe I should be a twelve-year-old with braces, she decided, then shook her head at her own thought pattern. She didn't want Shade's affection. His respect, yes.

It wasn't until after dinner that she realized she was wrong. She wanted a great deal more.

It was the last leisurely evening before the group separated. On the front porch they watched the first stars come out and listened to the first night sounds begin. By that time the next evening, Shade and Bryan would be in Colorado.

Lee and Hunter sat on the porch swing with Sarah nestled between them. Shade stretched out in a chair just to the side, relaxed, a little tired, and mentally satisfied after his long hours in the darkroom. Still, as he sat talking easily to the Browns, he realized that he'd needed this visit as much as, perhaps more than Bryan.

He'd had a simple childhood. Until these past days, he'd nearly forgotten just how simple, and just how solid. The things that had happened to him as an adult had blocked a great deal of it out. Now, without consciously realizing it, Shade was drawing some of it back.

Bryan sat on the first step, leaning back against a post. She joined in the conversation or distanced herself from it as she chose. There was nothing important being said, and the easiness of the conversation made the scene that much more appealing. A moth battered itself against the porch light, crickets called and the breeze rippled through the full leaves of the surrounding trees. The sounds made a soothing conversation of their own.

She liked the way Hunter had his arm across the back of the swing. Though he spoke to Shade, his fingers ran lightly over his wife's hair. His daughter's head rested against his chest, but once in a while, she'd reach a hand over to Lee's stomach as if to test for movement. Though she hadn't been consciously setting the scene, it grew in front of her eyes. Unable to resist, Bryan slipped inside.

When she returned a few moments later, she had her camera, tripod and light stand.

"Oh boy." Sarah took one look and straightened primly. "Bryan's going to take our picture."

"No posing," Bryan told her with a grin. "Just keep talking," she continued before anyone could protest. "Pretend I'm not even here. It's so perfect," she began to mutter to herself as she set up. "I don't know why I didn't see it before."

"Let me give you a hand."

Bryan glanced up at Shade in surprise and had nearly refused before she stopped the words. It was the first time he'd made any attempt to work with her. Whether it was a gesture to her or to the affection he'd come to feel for her friends, she wouldn't toss it back at him. Instead she smiled and handed him her light meter.

"Give me a reading, will you?"

They worked together as though they'd been doing so for years. Another surprise, for both of them. She adjusted her light, already calculating her exposure as Shade gave her the readings. Satisfied, Bryan checked the angle and framing through the viewfinder, then stepped back and let Shade take her place.

"Perfect." If she was looking for a lazy summer evening and a family content with it and one another, she could've done no better. Stepping back, Shade leaned against the wall of the house. Without thinking about it, he continued to help by distracting the trio on the swing.

"What do you want, Sarah?" he began as Bryan moved behind the camera again. "A baby brother or a sister?"

As she considered, Sarah forgot her enchantment with being photographed. "Well…" Her hand moved to Lee's stomach again. Lee's hand closed over it spontaneously. Bryan clicked the shutter. "Maybe a brother," she decided. "My cousin says a little sister can be a real pain."

As Sarah spoke Lee leaned her head back, just slightly, until it rested on Hunter's arm. His fingers brushed her hair again. Bryan felt the emotion well up in her and blur her vision. She took the next shot blindly.

Had she always wanted that? she wondered as she continued to shoot. The closeness, the contentment that came with commitment and intimacy? Why had it waited to slam into her now, when her feelings toward Shade were already tangled and much too complicated? She blinked her eyes clear and opened the shutter just as Lee turned her head to laugh at something Hunter said.

Relationship, she thought as the longing rose up in her. Not the easy, careless friendships she'd permitted herself, but a solid, demanding, sharing relationship. That was what she saw through the viewfinder. That was what she discovered she needed for herself. When she straightened from the camera, Shade was beside her.

"Something wrong?"

She shook her head and reached over to switch off the light. "Perfect," she announced with a casualness that cost her. She gave the family on the swing a smile. "I'll send you a print as soon as we stop and develop again."

She was trembling. Shade was close enough to see it. He turned and dealt with the camera and tripod himself. "I'll take this up for you."

She turned to tell him no, but he was already carrying it inside. "I'd better pack my gear," she said to Hunter and Lee. "Shade likes to leave at uncivilized hours."

When she went inside, Lee leaned her head against Hunter's arm again. "They'll be fine," he told her. "She'll be fine."

Lee glanced toward the doorway. "Maybe."

Shade carried Bryan's equipment up to the bedroom she'd been using and waited. The moment she came in with the light, he turned to her. "What's wrong?"

Bryan opened the case and packed her stand and light. "Nothing. Why?"

"You were trembling." Impatient, Shade took her arm and turned her around. "You're still trembling."

"I'm tired." In its way, it was true. She was tired of having her emotions sneak up on her.

"Don't play games with me, Bryan. I'm better at it than you."

God, could he have any idea just how much she wanted to be held at that moment? Would he have any way of understanding how much she'd give if only he'd hold her now? "Don't push it, Shade."

She should've known he wouldn't listen. With one hand he cupped her chin and held her face steady. The eyes that saw a great deal more than he was entitled to looked into hers. "Tell me."

"No." She said it quietly. If she'd been angry, insulted, cold, he'd have dug until he'd had it all. He couldn't fight her this way.

"All right." He backed off, dipping his hands into his pockets. He'd felt something out on the porch, something that had pulled at him, offered itself to him. If she'd made one move, the slightest move, he might have given her more at that moment than either of them could imagine. "Maybe you should get some sleep. We'll leave at seven."

"Okay." Deliberately she turned away to pack up the rest of her gear. "I'll be ready."

He was at the door before he felt compelled to turn around again. "Bryan, I saw your prints. They're exceptional."

She felt the first tears stream down her face and was appalled. Since when did she cry because someone acknowledged her talent? Since when did she tremble because a picture she was taking spoke to her personally?

She pressed her lips together for a moment and continued to pack without turning around. "Thanks."

Shade didn't linger any longer. He closed the door soundlessly on his way out.

Chapter Six

By the time they'd passed through New Mexico and into Colorado, Bryan felt more in tune with herself. In part, she thought that the break in Oak Creek Canyon had given her too much time for introspection. Though she often relied heavily on just that in her work, there were times when it could be self-defeating.

At least that's what she'd been able to convince herself of after she and Shade had picked up the routine of drive and shoot and drive some more.

They weren't looking for cities and major events on this leg. They sought out small, unrecognizable towns and struggling ranches. Families that worked with the land and one another to make ends meet. For them, summer was a time of hard, endless work to prepare for the rigors of winter. It wasn't all fun, all games, all sun and sand. It was migrant workers waiting to pick August peaches, and gardens being weeded and tended to offset the expense of winter vegetables.

They didn't consider Denver, but chose instead places like Antonito. They didn't go after the big, sprawling cattle spreads, but the smaller, more personal operations.

Bryan had her first contact with a cattle branding on a dusty little ranch called the Bar T. Her preconception of sweaty, loose-limbed cowboys rounding 'em up and heading 'em out wasn't completely wrong. It just hadn't included the more basic aspects of branding—such as the smell of burned flesh and the splash of blood as potential bulls were turned into little steers.

She was, she'd discovered as her stomach heaved, a city girl at heart.

But they got their pictures. Cowboys with bandannas over their faces and spurs on their boots. Some of them laughed, some of them swore. All of them worked.

She learned the true meaning of work horse as she watched the men push their mounts through their paces. The sweat of a horse was a heavy, rich smell. It hung thickly in the air with the sweat of men.

Bryan considered her best shot a near classic study of a man taking hold of his leisure time with both hands. The young cowboy was rangy and ruddy, which made him perfect for what she was after. His chambray shirt was dark with patches of sweat down the front, down the back and spreading from under the arms. More sweat mixed with dust ran down his face. His work boots were creased and caked with grime. The back pocket of his jeans was worn from the constant rub against a round can of chewing tobacco. With his hat tilted back and his bandanna tied loosely around his throat, he straddled the fence and lifted an icy can of beer to his lips.

Bryan thought when the picture was printed you'd almost be able to see his Adam's apple move as he swallowed. And every woman who looked at it, she was certain, would be half in love. He was the mystic, the swashbuckler, the last of the knights. Having that picture in her camera nearly made up for almost losing her lunch over the branding.

She'd seen Shade hone right in on it and knew his pictures would be gritty, hard and detailed. Yet she'd also seen him focusing in on a young boy of eleven or twelve as he'd ridden in his first roundup with all the joy and innocence peculiar to a boy of that age. His choice had surprised her because he rarely went for the lighter touch. It was also, unfortunately for her state of mind, something else she could like him for. There were others.

He hadn't made any comment when she'd turned green and had distanced herself for a time from what was going on in the small enclosed corral where calves bawled for their mothers and let out long, surprised wails when knife and iron were applied. He hadn't said a word when she'd sat down in the shade until she'd been certain her stomach would stay calm. Nor had he said a word when he'd handed her a cold drink. Neither had she.

That night they camped on Bar T land. Shade had given her space since they'd left Arizona because she suddenly seemed to need it. Oddly, he found he didn't. In the beginning, it had always been Bryan who'd all but forced him into conversations when he'd have been content to drive in silence for hours. Now he wanted to talk to her, to hear her laugh, to watch the way her hands moved when she became enthusiastic about a certain point. Or to watch the way she stretched, easily, degree by inching degree as her voice slowed.

Something undefinable had shifted in both of them during their time in Oak Creek. Bryan had become remote when she'd always been almost too open for his comfort. He found he wanted her company when he'd always been solitary. He wanted, though he didn't fully comprehend why, her friendship. It was a shift he wasn't certain he cared for, or even understood. In any case, because the opposing shifts had happened in both of them simultaneously, it brought them no closer.

Shade had chosen the open space near a fast-running creek for a campsite for no reason other than it appealed to him. Bryan immediately saw other possibilities.

"Look, I'm going down to wash off." She was as dusty as the cowboys she'd focused on all afternoon. It occurred to her, not altogether pleasantly, that she might smell a bit too much like the horses she'd watched. "It's probably freezing, so I'll make it fast and you can have a turn."

Shade pried the top off a beer. Perhaps they hadn't rounded up cattle, but they'd been on their feet and in the sun for almost eight hours. "Take your time."

Bryan grabbed a towel and a cake of soap and dashed off. The sun was steadily dropping behind the mountains to the west. She knew enough of camping by now to know how quickly the air would cool once the sun went down. She didn't want to be wet and naked when it did.

She didn't bother to glance around before she stripped off her shirt. They were far enough away from the ranch house that none of the men would wander out that way at sunset. Shade and she had already established the sanctity of privacy without exchanging a word on the subject.

Right now, she thought as she wiggled out of her jeans, the cowboys they'd come to shoot were probably sitting down to an enormous meal—red meat and potatoes, she mused. Hot biscuits with plenty of butter. Lord knows they deserved it after the day they'd put in. And me, too, she decided, though she and Shade were making do with cold sandwiches and a bag of chips.

Slim, tall and naked, Bryan took a deep breath of the pine-scented air. Even a city girl, she thought as she paused a moment to watch the sunset, could appreciate all this.

Gingerly she stepped into the cold knee-high water and began to rinse off the dust. Strange, she didn't mind the chill as much as she once had. The drive across America was bound to leave its mark. She was glad of it.

No one really wanted to stay exactly the same throughout life. If her outlook changed and shifted as they traveled, she was fortunate. The assignment was giving her more than the chance for professional exposure and creative expression. It was giving her experiences. Why else had she become a photographer but to see things and understand them?

Yet she didn't understand Shade any better now than when they'd started out. Had she tried? In some ways, she thought, as she glided the soap over her arms. Until what she saw and understood began to affect her too deeply and too personally. Then she'd backed off fast.

She didn't like to admit it. Bryan shivered and began to wash more swiftly. The sun was nearly set. Self-preservation, she reminded herself. Perhaps her image was one of take what comes and make the best of it, but she had her phobias as well. And she was entitled to them.

It had been a long time since she'd been hurt, and that was because of her own deceptively simple maneuvering. If she stood at a crossroads and had two routes, one smooth, the other rocky with a few pits, she'd take the smooth one. Maybe it was less admirable, but she'd always felt you ended up in the same place with less energy expended. Shade Colby was a rocky road.

In any case, it wasn't just a matter of her choice. They could have an affair—a physically satisfying, emotionally shallow affair. It worked well for a great many people. But...

He didn't want to be involved with her any more than she did with him. He was attracted, just as she was, but he wasn't offering her any more than that. If he ever did... She dropped that line of thought like a stone. Speculation wasn't always healthy.

The important thing was that she felt more like herself again. She was pleased with the work she'd done since they'd left Arizona and was looking forward to crossing over into Kansas the next day. The assignment, as they'd both agreed from the outset, was the first priority.

Wheat fields and tornados, she thought with a grin. Follow the yellow brick road. That was what Kansas brought to her mind. She knew better now, and looked forward to finding the reality. Bryan was beginning to enjoy having her preconceptions both confirmed and blown to bits.

That was for tomorrow. Right now it was dusk and she was freezing.

Agile, she scrambled up the small bank and reached for the towel. Shade could wash up while she stuffed herself with whatever was handy in the cupboards. She pulled on a long-sleeved oversize shirt and reached up to button it. That's when she saw the eyes.

For a moment she only stared with her hands poised at the top button. Then she saw there was more to it than a pair of narrow yellow eyes peering out of the lowering light. There was a sleek, muscled body and a set of sharp, white teeth only a narrow creek bed away.

Bryan took two steps back, tripped over her own tangled jeans and let out a scream that might've been heard in the next county.

Shade was stretched out in a folding chair beside the small campfire he'd built on impulse. He'd enjoyed himself that day—the rough and ready atmosphere, the baking sun and cold beer. He'd always admired the comaraderie that went hand in hand with people who work outdoors.

He needed the city—it was in his blood. For the most part, he preferred the impersonal aspects of people rushing to their own places, in their own time. But it helped to touch base with other aspects of life from time to time.

He could see now, even after only a few weeks on the road, that he'd been getting stale. He hadn't had the challenge of his early years. That get-the-shot-and-stay-alive sort of challenge. He didn't want it. But he'd let himself become too complacent with what he'd been doing.

This assignment had given him the chance to explore himself as well as his country. He thought of his partner with varying degrees of puzzlement and interest. She wasn't nearly as simple or laid-back as he'd originally believed. Still, she was nearly 180 degrees removed from him. He was beginning to understand her. Slowly, but he was beginning to.

She was sensitive, emotional and inherently kind. He was rarely kind because he was careful not to be. She was comfortable with herself, easily amused and candid. He'd learned long ago that candor can jump back on you with teeth.

But he wanted her—because she was different or in spite of it, he wanted her. Forcing himself to keep his hands off her in all the days and nights that had passed since that light, interrupted kiss in Hunter Brown's driveway was beginning to wear on him. He had his control to thank for the fact that he'd been able to, the control that he honed so well that it was nearly a prison.

Shade tossed his cigarette into the fire and leaned back. He wouldn't lose that control, or break out of that prison, but that didn't mean that sooner or later he and Bryan wouldn't be lovers. He meant it to happen. He would simply bide his time until it happened his way. As long as he was holding the reins, he wouldn't steer himself into the mire.

When he heard her scream, a dozen agonizing images rushed into his head, images that he'd seen and lived through, images that only someone who had could conjure up. He was out of the chair and running before he'd fully realized they were only memories.

When he got to her, Bryan was scrambling up from the tumble she'd taken. The last thing she expected was to be hauled up and crushed against Shade. The last thing she expected was exactly what she needed. Gasping for air, she clung to him.

"What happened?" Her own panic muffled her ears to the thread of panic in his voice. "Bryan, are you hurt?"

"No, no. It scared me, but it ran away." She pushed her face against his shoulder and just breathed. "Oh God, Shade."

"What?" Gripping her by the elbows, he pulled her back far enough to see her face. "What scared you?"

"A cat."

He wasn't amused. His fear turned to fury, tangibly enough that Bryan could see the latter even before he cursed her. "Damn it! What kind of fool are you?" he demanded. "Letting out a scream like that over a cat."

She drew air in and out, in and out, and concentrated on her anger—genuine fear was something she didn't care for. "Not a house cat," she snapped. She was still shaken, but not enough to sit back and be called a fool. "It was one of those . . . I don't know." She lifted a hand to push at her hair and dropped it again when it trembled. "I have to sit down." She did so with a plop on the grass.

"A bobcat?" Calmer, Shade crouched down beside her.

"I don't know. Bobcat, cougar—I wouldn't know the difference. It was a hell of a lot bigger than any tabby." She lowered her head to her knees. Maybe she'd been frightened before in her life, but she couldn't remember anything to compare with this. "He just stood over there, staring at me. I thought—I thought he was going to jump over the creek. His teeth . . ." She shuddered and shut her eyes. "Big," she managed, no longer caring if she sounded like a simple-minded fool. "Real big."

"He's gone now." His fury turned inward. He should've known she wasn't the kind of woman who jumped at shadows. He knew what it was to be afraid and to feel helpless with it. This time he cursed himself as he slipped an arm around her. "The way you screamed, he's ten miles away and still running."

Bryan nodded but kept her face buried against her knees. "I guess he wasn't that big, but they look different out of the zoo. I just need a minute to pull myself together."

"Take your time."

He found he didn't mind offering comfort, though it was something he hadn't done in a long time. The air was cool, the night still. He could hear the sound of the water rushing by in the creek. For a moment he had a quick flash of the Browns's porch, of the easy, family portrait on the swing. He felt a touch of the same contentment here with his arm around Bryan and night closing in.

Overhead a hawk screeched, out for its first flight of the night. Bryan jolted.

"Easy," Shade murmured. He didn't laugh at her reaction, or even smile. He soothed.

"I guess I'm a little jumpy." With a nervous laugh, she lifted her hand to push at her hair again. It wasn't until then that Shade realized she was naked beneath the open, billowing shirt.

The sight of her slim, supple body beneath the thin fluttering material sent the contentment he'd felt skyrocketing into need. A need, he discovered only in that instant, that was somehow exclusively for her—not just for a woman with a lovely face, a desirable body, but for Bryan.

"Maybe we should get back and..." She turned her head and found her eyes only inches from his. In his, she saw everything he felt. When she started to speak again, he shook his head.

No words. No words now. Only needs, only feelings. He wanted that with her. As his mouth closed over hers, he gave her no choice but to want it as well.

Sweetness? Where had it come from and how could she possibly turn away from it? They'd been together nearly a month but she'd never suspected he had sweetness in him. Nor had she known just how badly she'd needed to find it there.

His mouth demanded, but so slowly, so subtly that she was giving before she was aware of it. Once she'd given, she couldn't take away again. She felt his hand, warm and firm on her bare skin, but she sighed in pleasure, not in protest. She'd wanted him to touch her, had waited for it, had denied her waiting. Now she leaned closer. There'd be no denying.

He'd known she'd feel like this—slim, strong, smooth. A hundred times, he'd imagined it. He hadn't forgotten that she'd taste like this—warm, tempting, generous. A hundred times he'd tried not to remember.

This time she smelled of the creek, fresh and cool. He could bury his face in her throat and smell the summer night on her. He kissed her slowly, leaving her lips for her throat, her throat for her shoulder. As he lingered there, he gave himself the pleasure of discovering her body with his fingertips.

It was torture. Exquisite. Agonizing. Irresistible. Bryan wanted it to go on, and on and on. She drew him closer, loving the hard, lean feel of his body against hers, the brush of his clothes against her skin, the whisper of his breath across it. And through it all, the quick, steady beat of his heart near hers.

She could smell the work of the day on him, the faint tang of healthy sweat, the traces of dust he hadn't yet washed off. It excited her with memories of the way his muscles had bunched beneath his shirt when he'd climbed onto a fence for a better angle. She could remember exactly how he'd looked then, though she'd pretended to herself that she hadn't seen, hadn't needed to.

She wanted his strength. Not the muscles, but the inner strength she'd sensed in him from the start. The strength that had carried him through what he'd seen, what he'd lived with.

Yet wasn't it that strength that helped to harden him, to separate him emotionally from the people around him? With her mind whirling, her body pulsing, she struggled to find the answer she needed.

Wants weren't enough. Hadn't she told him so herself? God, she wanted him. Her bones were melting from the desire for him. But it wasn't enough. She only wished she knew what was.

"Shade..." Even when she tried to speak he cut her off with another long, draining kiss.

She wanted him to drain her. Mind, body, soul. If he did, there'd be no question and no need for answers. But the questions were there. Even as she held him to her, they were there.

"Shade," she began again.

"I want to make love with you." He lifted his head and his eyes were so dark, so intense it was almost impossible to believe his hands were so gentle. "I want to feel your skin under my hand, feel your heart race, watch your eyes."

The words were quiet, incredibly calm when his eyes were so passionate. More than the passion and demand in his eyes, the words frightened her.

"I'm not ready for this." She barely managed the words as she drew away from him.

He felt the needs rise and the anger begin. It took all his skill to control both. "Are you saying you don't want me?"

"No." She shook her head as she drew her shirt together. When had it become so cold? she wondered. "No, lying's foolish."

"So's backing away from something we both want to happen."

"I'm not sure I do. I can't be logical about this, Shade." She gathered her clothes quickly and hugged them against her as she stood. "I can't think something like this through step by step the way you do. If I could, it'd be different, but I can only go with my feelings, my instincts.''

There was a deadly calm around him when he rose. The control he'd nearly forfeited to her was back in place. Once more he accepted the prison he'd built himself. ''And?''

She shivered without knowing if it was from the cold without or the cold within. ''And my feelings tell me I need more time.'' When she looked up at him again, her face was honest, her eyes eloquent. ''Maybe I do want this to happen. Maybe I'm just a little afraid of how much I want you.''

He didn't like her use of the word afraid. She made him feel responsible, obliged. Defensive. ''I've no intention of hurting you.''

She gave herself a moment. Her breathing was easier even if her pulse was still unsteady. Whether he knew it or not, Shade had already given her the distance she needed to resist him. Now she could look at him, calmer. Now she could think more clearly.

''No, I don't think you do, but you could, and I have a basic fear of bruises. Maybe I'm an emotional coward. It's not a pretty thought, but it might be true.'' With a sigh, she lifted both hands to her hair and pushed it back. ''Shade, we've a bit more than two months left on the road. I can't afford to spend it being torn up inside because of you. My instincts tell me you could very easily do that to me whether you planned on it or not.''

She knew how to back a man into a corner, he thought in frustration. He could press, relieve the knot she'd tightened in his stomach. And by doing so, he'd run the risk of having her words echo back at him for a long time to come. It'd only taken a few words from her to remind him what it felt like to be responsible for someone else.

"Go back to the van," he told her, turning away to strip off this shirt. "I have to clean up."

She started to speak, then realized there was nothing more she could say. Instead she left him to follow the thin moonlit trail back to the van.

Chapter Seven

Wheat fields. Bryan didn't see her preconception slashed as they drove through the Midwest, but reinforced. Kansas was wheat fields.

Whatever else Bryan saw as they crossed the state, it was the endless, rippling gold grass that captivated her, first and last. Color, texture, shape, form. Emotion. There were towns, of course, cities with modern buildings and plush homes, but in seeing basic Americana, grain against sky, Bryan saw it all.

Some might have found the continuous spread of sunripened grain waving, acre after acre, monotonous. Not Bryan. This was a new experience for a woman of the city. There were no jutting mountains, no glossy towering buildings, no looping freeways to break the lines. Here was space, just as awesome as the terrain of Arizona, but lusher, and somehow calmer. She could look at it and wonder.

In the fields of wheat and acres of corn, Bryan saw the heart and the sweat of the country. It wasn't always an idyllic scene. There were insects, dirt, grimy machinery. People worked here with their hands, with their backs.

In the cities she saw the pace and energy. On the farms, she saw a schedule that would have made a corporate executive wilt. Year after year, the farmer gave himself to the land and waited for the land to give back.

With the right angle, the proper light, she could photograph a wheat field and make it seem endless, powerful. With evening shadows, she could give a sense of serenity and continuity. It was only grass after all, only stalks growing to be cut down, processed, used. But the grain had a life and a beauty of its own. She wanted to show it as she saw it.

Shade saw the tenuous, inescapable dependence of man on nature. The planter, keeper and harvester of the wheat was irrevocably tied to the land. It was both his freedom and his prison. The man riding the tractor in the Kansas sunlight, damp with healthy sweat, lean from years of labor, was as dependent on the land as the land was on him. Without man, the wheat might grow wild, it might flourish, but then it would wither and die. It was the tie Shade sensed, and the tie he meant to record.

Still, perhaps for the first time since they'd left L.A., he and Bryan weren't shooting as separate entities. They might not have realized it yet, but their feelings, perceptions and needs were drawing them closer to the same mark.

They made each other think. How did she see this scene? How did he feel about this setting? Where before each of them had considered their photographs separately, now subtly, unconsciously, they began to do two things that would improve the final result: compete and consult.

They'd spent a day and a night in Dodge City for the Fourth of July celebrations in what had once been a Wild West town. Bryan thought of Wyatt Earp, of Doc Holliday and the desperadoes who had once ridden through town, but she'd been drawn to the street parade that might've been in Anytown, U.S.A.

It was here, caught up in the pageantry and the flavor, that she'd asked Shade his opinion of the right angle for shooting a horse and rider, and he in turn had taken her advice on capturing a tiny, bespangled majorette.

The step they'd taken had been lost in the moment to both of them. But they'd stood side by side on the curb as the parade had passed, music blaring, batons flying. Their pictures had been different—Shade had looked for the overview of holiday parades while Bryan had wanted individual reactions. But they'd stood side by side.

Bryan's feelings for Shade had become more complex, more personal. When the change had begun or how, she couldn't say. But because her work was most often a direct result of her emotions, the pictures she took began to reflect both the complexity and the intimacy. Their view of the same wheat field might be radically different, but Bryan was determined that when their prints were set side by side, hers would have equal impact.

She'd never been an aggressive person. It just wasn't her style. But Shade had tapped a need in her to compete—as a photographer, and as a woman. If she had to travel in close quarters for weeks with a man who ruffled her professional feathers and stirred her feminine needs, she had to deal with him directly—on both counts. Directly, she decided, but in her own fashion and her own time. As the days went on, Bryan wondered if it would be possible to have both success and Shade without losing something vital.

She was so damn calm! It drove him crazy. Every day, every hour they spent together pushed Shade closer to the edge. He wasn't used to wanting anyone so badly. He didn't enjoy finding out he could, and that there was nothing he could do about it. Bryan put him in the position of needing, then having to deny himself. There were times he nearly believed she did so purposely. But he'd never known anyone less likely to scheme than Bryan. She wouldn't think of it—and if she did, she'd consider it too much bother.

Even now, as they drove through the Kansas twilight, she was stretched out in the seat beside him, sound asleep. It was one of the rare times she'd left her hair loose. Full, wavy and lush, it was muted to a dull gold in the lowering light. The sun had given her skin all the color it needed. Her body was relaxed, loose like her hair. Shade wondered if he'd ever had the capability to let his mind and body go so enviably limp. Was it that that tempted him, that drove at him? Was he simply pushed to find that spark of energy she could turn on and off at will? He wanted to set it to life. For himself.

Temptation. The longer he held himself back, the more intense it became. To have her. To explore her. To absorb her. When he did—he no longer used the word if— what cost would there be? Nothing was free.

Once, he thought as she sighed in sleep. Just once. His way. Perhaps the cost would be high, but he wouldn't be the one to pay it. His emotions were trained and disciplined. They wouldn't be touched. There wasn't a woman alive who could make him hurt.

His body and his mind tensed as Bryan slowly woke. Groggy and content to be so, she yawned. The scent of smoke and tobacco stung the air. On the radio was low, mellow jazz. The windows were half open so that when she shifted, the slap of wind woke her more quickly than she'd have liked.

It was fully dark now. Surprised, Bryan stretched and stared out the window at a moon half covered by clouds. 'It's late,'' she said on another yawn. The first thing she remembered as her mind cleared of sleep was that they hadn't eaten. She pressed a hand to her stomach. "Dinner?"

He glanced at her just long enough to see her shake back her hair. It rippled off her shoulders and down her back. As he watched he had to fight back the urge to touch it. "I want to get over the border tonight."

She heard it in his voice—the tension, the annoyance. Bryan didn't know what had prompted it, nor at the moment did she want to. Instead, she lifted a brow. If he was in a hurry to get to Oklahoma and was willing to drive into the night to get there, it was his business. She'd stocked a cabinet in the back of the van with a few essentials just for moments like this. Bryan started to haul herself out of her seat when she heard the long blare of a horn and the rev of an engine.

The scarred old Pontiac had a hole in the muffler you could've tossed a baseball through. The sound of the engine clattered like a badly tuned plane. It swerved around the van at a dangerous speed, fishtailed, then bolted ahead, radio blaring. As Shade swore, Bryan got a glimpse that revealed the dilapidated car was packed with kids.

"Saturday night in July," she commented.

"Idiots," he said between his teeth as he watched the taillights weave.

"Yeah." She frowned as she watched the car barrel ahead, smoke streaming. "They were just kids, I hope they don't..."

Even as she thought it, it happened. The driver decided to press his luck by passing another car over the double yellow lines. The truck coming toward him laid on the horn and swerved. Bryan felt her blood freeze.

Shade was already hitting the brakes as the Pontiac screeched back in its own lane. But it was out of control. Skidding sideways, the Pontiac kissed the fender of the car it had tried to pass, then flipped into a telephone pole.

The sound of screaming tires, breaking glass and smashing metal whirled in her head. Bryan was up and out of the van before Shade had brought it to a complete stop. She could hear a girl screaming, others weeping. Even as the sounds shuddered through her, she told herself it meant they were alive.

The door on the passenger's side was crushed against the telephone pole. Bryan rushed to the driver's side and wrenched at the handle. She smelled the blood before she saw it. "Good God," she whispered as she managed to yank the door open on the second try. Then Shade was beside her, shoving her aside.

"Get some blankets out of the van," he ordered without looking at her. It had only taken him one glance at the driver to tell him it wasn't going to be pretty. He shifted enough to block Bryan's view, then reached in to check the pulse in the driver's throat as he heard her run back to the van. Alive, he thought, then blocked out everything but what had to be done. He worked quickly.

The driver was unconscious. The gash on his head was serious, but it didn't worry Shade as much as the probability of internal injuries. And nothing worried him as much as the smell of gas that was beginning to sweeten the air. Under other circumstances, Shade would've been reluctant to move the boy. Now there was no choice. Locking his arms under the boy's arms, Shade hauled him out. Even as Shade began to drag him, the driver of the truck ran over and took the boy's legs.

"Got a CB in the truck," he told Shade breathlessly. "Called for an ambulance."

With a nod, Shade laid the boy down. Bryan was already there with the first blanket.

"Stay here. The car's going to go up." He said it calmly. Without a backward glance he went back to the crippled Pontiac.

Terror jolted through her. Within seconds, Bryan was at the car beside him, helping to pull the others out of the wreck.

"Get back to the van," Shade shouted at her as Bryan half carried a sobbing girl. "Stay there."

Bryan spoke soothingly, covered the girl with a blanket then rushed back to the car. The last passenger was also unconscious. A boy, Bryan saw, of no more than sixteen. She had to half crawl into the car to reach him. By the time she'd dragged him to the open door, she was drenched and exhausted. Both Shade and the truck driver carried the other injured passengers. Shade had just set a young girl on the grass when he turned and saw Bryan struggling with the last victim.

Fear was instant and staggering. Even as he started to run, his imagination worked on him. In his mind, Shade could see the flash of explosion, hear the sound of bursting metal and shattering, flying glass. He knew exactly what it would smell like the moment the gas ignited. When he reached Bryan, Shade scooped up the unconscious boy as though he were weightless.

"Run!" he shouted at her. Together, they raced away from the Pontiac.

Bryan didn't see the explosion. She heard it, but more, she felt it. The whoosh of hot air slammed into her back and sent her sprawling onto the grassy shoulder of the road. There was a whistle of metal as something hot and twisted and lethal flew overhead. One of the teenagers screamed and buried her face in her hands.

Stunned, Bryan lay prone a moment waiting to catch her breath. Over the sound of fire, she could hear the whine of sirens.

"Are you hurt!" Shade half dragged her up to her knees. He'd seen the flying slice of metal whiz by her head. Hands that had been rock steady moments before trembled as they gripped her.

"No." Bryan shook her head, and finding her balance turned to the whimpering girl beside her. A broken arm, she realized as she tucked the blanket under the girl's chin. And the cut on her temple would need stitches. "Take it easy," Bryan murmured, pulling out a piece of gauze from the first-aid box she'd brought from the van. "You're going to be fine. The ambulance is coming. Can you hear it?"

As she spoke she pressed the gauze against the wound to stop the bleeding. Her voice was calm, her fingers trembled.

"Bobby." Tears ran down the girl's face as she clung to Bryan. "Is Bobby all right? He was driving."

Bryan glanced over and looked directly at Shade before she lowered her gaze to the unconscious boy. "He's going to be fine," she said and felt helpless.

Six young, careless children, she thought as she scanned those sitting or lying on the grass. The driver of the other car sat dazedly across from them, holding a rag to the cut on his own head. For a moment, a long still moment, the night was quiet—warm, almost balmy. Stars were brilliant overhead. Moonlight was strong and lovely. Thirty feet away, what was left of the Pontiac crackled with flame. Bryan slipped her arm around the shoulders of the girl and watched the lights of the ambulance speed up the road.

As the paramedics began to work, another ambulance and the fire department were called. For twenty minutes, Bryan sat by the young girl, talking to her, holding her hand while her injuries were examined and tended to.

Her name was Robin. She was seventeen. Of the six teenagers in the car, her boyfriend, Bobby, was the oldest at nineteen. They'd only been celebrating summer vacation.

As Bryan listened and soothed, she glanced up to see Shade calmly setting his camera. Astonished, she watched as he carefully focused and framed in the injured. Dispassionately, he recorded the scene of the accident, the victims and what was left of the car. As astonishment faded, Bryan felt the fury bubble inside her. When Robin was carried to the second ambulance, Bryan sprang up.

"What the hell are you doing?" She grabbed his shoulder, spoiling a shot. Still calm, Shade turned to her and gave her one quick study.

She was pale. Her eyes showed both strain and fury. And, he thought, a dull sheen of shock. For the first time since he'd known her, Shade saw how tense her body could be. "I'm doing my job," he said simply and lifted the camera again.

"Those kids are bleeding!" Bryan grabbed his shoulder again, swinging herself around until she was face-to-face with him. "They've got broken bones. They're hurt and they're frightened. Since when is your job taking pictures of their pain?"

"Since I picked up a camera for pay." Shade let the camera swing by its strap. He'd gotten enough in any case. He didn't like the feeling in his own stomach, the tension behind his eyes. Most of all, he didn't like the look in Bryan's as she stared at him. Disgust. He shrugged it off.

"You're only willing to take pictures of fun in the sun for this assignment, Bryan. You saw the car, those kids. That's part of it too. Part of life. If you can't handle it, you'd better stick to your celebrity shots and leave the real world alone."

He'd taken two steps toward the van when Bryan was on him again. She might avoid confrontations as a matter of habit, take the line of least resistance as often as possible, but there were times when she'd fight. When she did, she used everything.

"I can handle it." She wasn't pale any longer; her face glowed with anger. Her eyes gleamed with it. "What I can't handle are the vultures who love picking at bones, making a profit off misery in the name of art. There were six people in that car. *People*," she repeated, hissing at him. "Maybe they were foolish, maybe they deserved what happened, but I'll be damned if I'm going to judge. Do you think it makes you a better photographer, a better artist because you're cold enough, you're *professional* enough to freeze their pain on printing paper? Is this the way you look for another Pulitzer nomination?"

She was crying now, too angry, too churned up by what she'd seen to be aware of the tears streaming down her cheeks. Yet somehow the tears made her look stronger. They thickened her voice and gave it impact. "I'll tell you what it makes you," she went on when Shade remained silent. "It makes you empty. Whatever compassion you were born with died somewhere along the way, Shade. I'm sorry for you."

She left him standing in the middle of the road by the shell of the car.

* * *

It was nearly 3:00 A.M. Shade had learned that the mind was at its most helpless in those early hours of the morning. The van was dark and quiet, parked in a small campground just over the Oklahoma border. He and Bryan hadn't exchanged a word since the accident. Each had prepared for bed in silence, and though both of them had lain awake for some time, neither had spoken. Now they slept, but only Bryan slept dreamlessly.

There'd been a time, during the first months after his return from Cambodia, that Shade had had the dream regularly. Over the years it had come to him less and less. Often he could force himself awake and fight the dream off before it really took hold. But now, in the tiny Oklahoma campground, he was powerless.

He knew he was dreaming. The moment the figures and shapes began to form in his mind, Shade understood it wasn't real—that it wasn't real any longer. It didn't stop the panic or the pain. The Shade Colby in the dream would go through the same motions he'd gone through all those years ago, leading to the same end. And in the dream there were no soft lines, no mists to lessen the impact. He saw it as it had happened, in strong sunlight.

Shade came out of the hotel and onto the street with Dave, his assistant. Between them, they carried all their luggage and equipment. They were going home. After four months of hard, often dangerous work in a city torn, ravaged and smoldering, they were going home. It had occurred to Shade that they were calling it close—but he'd called it close before. Every day they stayed on added to the risk of getting out at all. But there'd always been one more picture to take, one more statement to make. And there'd been Sung Lee.

She'd been so young, so eager, so wise. As a contact in the city, she'd been invaluable. She'd been just as invaluable to Shade personally. After a bumpy, unpleasant divorce from a wife who'd wanted more glamour and less reality, Shade had needed the long, demanding assignment. And he'd needed Sung Lee.

She was devoted, sweet, undemanding. When he'd taken her to bed, Shade had finally been able to block out the rest of the world and relax. His only regret in going back home was that she wouldn't leave her country.

As they'd stepped out on the street, Shade had been thinking of her. They'd said their goodbyes the night before, but he was thinking of her. Perhaps if he hadn't been he'd have sensed something. He'd asked himself that hundreds of times in the months that followed.

The city was quiet, but it wasn't peaceful. The tension in the air could erupt at any time. Those who were getting out were doing so in a hurry. Tomorrow, the next day, the doors might be closed. Shade took one last look around as they started toward their car. One last picture, he'd thought, of the calm before the storm.

A few careless words to Dave and he was alone, standing on the curb pulling his camera out of its case. He laughed as Dave swore and struggled with the luggage on his way to the car. Just one last picture. The next time he lifted his camera to shoot, it would be on American soil.

"Hey, Colby!" Young, grinning, Dave stood beside the car. He looked like a college student on spring break. "How about taking one of a future award-winning photographer on his way out of Cambodia?"

With a laugh, Shade lifted his camera and framed in his assistant. He remembered exactly the way he'd looked. Blond, tanned, a bit gangly with a crooked front tooth and a faded USC T-shirt.

He took the shot. Dave turned the key in the lock.

"Let's go home," his assistant yelled the instant before the car exploded.

"Shade. Shade!" Heart pounding, Bryan shook him. "Shade, wake up, it's a dream." He grabbed her hard enough to make bruises but she kept talking. "It's Bryan, Shade. You're having a dream. Just a dream. We're in Oklahoma, in your van. Shade." She took his face in her hands and felt the skin cold and damp. "Just a dream," she said quietly. "Try to relax. I'm right here."

He was breathing too quickly. Shade felt himself straining for air and forced himself to calm. God, he was cold. He felt the warmth of Bryan's skin under his hands, heard her voice, calm, low, soothing. With an oath he dropped back down again and waited for the shuddering to stop.

"I'll get you some water."

"Scotch."

"All right." The moonlight was bright enough. She found the plastic cup and the bottle and poured. Behind her, she heard the flare of his lighter and the hiss as it caught paper and tobacco. When Bryan turned, he was sitting up on the bunk, resting back against the side of the van. She had no experience with whatever trauma haunted Shade, but she did know how to soothe nerves. She handed him the drink, then without asking sat beside him. She waited until he'd taken the first sip.

"Better?"

He took another sip, a deeper one. "Yeah."

She touched his arm lightly, but the contact was made. "Tell me."

He didn't want to speak of it, not to anyone, not to her. Even as the refusal formed on his lips, she increased the grip on his arm.

"We'll both feel better if you do. Shade..." She had to wait again, this time for him to turn and look at her. Her heartbeat was steadier now, and so, as her fingers lay over his wrist, was his. But there was still a thin sheen of sweat drying on his skin. "Nothing gets better and goes away if you hold it in."

He'd held it in for years. It'd never gone away. Perhaps it never would. Maybe it was the quiet understanding in her voice, or the late hour, but he found himself talking.

He told her of Cambodia, and though his voice was flat, she could see it as he had. Ripe for explosion, crumbling, angry. Long, monotonous days punctuated by moments of terror. He told her how he'd reluctantly taken on an assistant and then learned to appreciate and enjoy the young man fresh out of college. And Sung Lee.

"We ran across her in a bar where most of the journalists hung out. It wasn't until a long time later that I put together just how convenient the meeting was. She was twenty, beautiful, sad. For nearly three months, she gave us leads she supposedly learned from a cousin who worked at the embassy."

"Were you in love with her?"

"No." He drew on his cigarette until there was nothing left but filter. "But I cared. I wanted to help her. And I trusted her."

He dropped his cigarette into an ashtray and concentrated on his drink. The panic was gone. He'd never realized he could talk about it calmly, think about it calmly. "Things were heating up and the magazine decided to pull its people out. We were going home. We were coming out of the hotel and I stopped to take a couple of shots. Like a tourist." He swore and drained the rest of the Scotch. "Dave got to the car first. It'd been booby-trapped."

"Oh, my God." Without realizing it, she moved closer to him.

"He was twenty-three. Carried a picture of the girl he was going to marry."

"I'm sorry." She laid her head against his shoulder, wound her arm around him. "I'm so sorry."

He braced himself against the flood of sympathy. He wasn't ready for it. "I tried to find Sung Lee. She was gone; her apartment was empty. It turned out that I'd been her assignment. The group she'd worked for had let things leak through so I'd relax and trust her. They'd intended to make a statement by blowing away an important American reporter. They'd missed me. An assistant photographer on his first overseas assignment didn't make any impact. The kid died for nothing."

And he'd watched the car explode, she thought. Just as he'd watched the car explode tonight. What had it done to him—then and now? Was that why, she wondered, he'd coolly taken out his camera and recorded it all? He was so determined not to feel.

"You blame yourself," she murmured. "You can't."

"He was a kid. I should've looked out for him."

"How?" She shifted so that they were face-to-face again. His eyes were dark, full of cold anger and frustration. She'd never forget just how they looked at that moment. "How?" she repeated. "If you hadn't stopped to take those pictures, you'd have gotten into the car with him. He'd still be dead."

"Yeah." Suddenly weary, Shade ran his hands over his face. The tension was gone, but not the bitterness. Perhaps that's what he was weary of.

"Shade, after the accident—"

"Forget it."

"No." This time she had his hand caught in hers. "You were doing what you had to, for your own reasons. I said I wouldn't judge those kids, but I was judging you. I'm sorry."

He didn't want her apology, but she gave it. He didn't want her to cleanse him, but she was washing away the guilt. He'd seen so much—too much—of the dark side of human nature. She was offering him the light. It tempted him and it terrified him.

"I'll never see things as you do," he murmured. After a moment's hesitation, he laced his fingers with hers. "I'll never be as tolerant."

Puzzled, she frowned as they stared at each other. "No, I don't think you will. I don't think you have to."

"You were right earlier when you said my compassion was dead. I haven't any." She started to speak but he shook his head. "I haven't any patience, very little sympathy."

Did he look at his own pictures? she wondered. Didn't he see the carefully harnessed emotion in them? But she said nothing, letting him make whatever point he needed to.

"I stopped believing in intimacy, genuine intimacy, permanency between two people, a long time ago. But I do believe in honesty."

She might've drawn away from him. There was something in his voice that warned her, but she stayed where she was. Their bodies were close. She could feel his heartbeat steady as hers began to race. "I think permanency works for some people." Was that her voice? she wondered, so calm, so practical. "I stopped looking for it for myself."

Isn't that what he'd wanted to hear? Shade looked down at their joined hands and wondered why her words left him dissatisfied. "Then it's understood that neither of us wants or needs promises."

Bryan opened her mouth, amazed that she wanted to object. She swallowed. "No promises," she managed. She had to think, had to have the distance to manage it. Deliberately she smiled. "I think we both could use some sleep, though."

He tightened his grip on her hand as she started to move. Honesty, he'd said. Though the words weren't easy for him, he'd say what he meant. He looked at her a long time. What was left of the moonlight showered her face and shadowed her eyes. Caught in his, her hand was steady. Her pulse wasn't.

"I need you, Bryan."

There were so many things he could have said, and to any of them she'd have had an answer. Wants—no, wants weren't enough. She'd already told him. Demands could be refused or shrugged off.

Needs. Needs were deeper, warmer, stronger. A need was enough.

He didn't move. He waited. Watching him, Bryan knew he'd let her take the step toward or away. Choices. He was a man who demanded them for himself, yet he was also capable of giving them. How could he know she'd had none the moment he'd spoken?

Slowly, she drew her hand from his. Just as slowly, she lifted both hands to his face and brought her mouth to his. With their eyes open, they shared a long, quiet kiss. It was a move that both offered and took.

She offered, with her hands light on his skin. She took, with her mouth warm and certain. He accepted. He gave. And then in the same instant, they both forgot the rules.

Her lashes fluttered down, her lips parted. Mindlessly he pulled her against him until their bodies were crushed close. She didn't resist, but went with him as they slid from the bunk and onto the rug.

She'd wanted this—the triumph and the weakness of being touched by him. She'd wanted the glory of letting herself go, of allowing her longings freedom. With his mouth hungry on hers, there was no need to think, no need to hold back what she'd wanted so desperately to give him. Only to him.

Take more. Her mind was reeling from the demands of her body. Take all. She could feel him tug at the wide neck of her sleep shirt until her shoulder was bare and vulnerable to his mouth. Still more. She skimmed her hands up his back, naked and warm from the night breeze flowing in the windows.

He wasn't easy as a lover. Hadn't she known it? There was no patience in him. Hadn't he told her? She'd known it before, but she was already aware that she'd never know relaxation with Shade. He drove her quickly, thoroughly. While she experienced all, she had no time to luxuriate in separate sensations. Masses of them swirled around, inside her.

Tastes...his lips, his skin—dark flavor. Scents... flowers, flesh—sweet and pungent. Textures...the nap of the rug rubbing against her legs, the hard brush of his palm, the soft warmth of his mouth. Sounds...her heartbeat pounding in her head, the murmur of her name in his whisper. She could see shadows, moonlight, the gleam of his eyes before his mouth took hers again. Everything merged and mixed together until they were one overpowering sensation. Passion.

He pulled the shirt lower until her arms were pinned. For a moment, she was helpless as he trailed his lips down her breast, pausing to taste, taste thoroughly, with lips, tongue, teeth. Some women would've found him merciless.

Perhaps it was the sound of her moan that made him linger when he was driven to hurry on. She was so slender, so smooth. The moonlight filtered in so that he could see where her tan gave way to paler, more vulnerable skin. Once he'd have turned away from vulnerability, knowing the dangers of it. Now it drew him—the softness of it. Her scent was there, clinging to the underside of her breast where he could taste as well as smell it. Sexy, tempting, subtle. It was as she was, and he was lost.

He felt his control slip, skid away from him. Ruthlessly, he brought it back. They would make love once— a hundred times that night—but he'd stay in control. As he was now, he thought as she arched under him. As he'd promised himself he would be, always. He would drive her, but he would not, could not, be driven by her.

Pulling the material down, he explored every inch of her mercilessly. He would show no mercy to either of them. Already she was beyond thought and he knew it. Her skin was hot and somehow softer with the heat; her scent intensified with it. He could run those hungry, openmouthed kisses wherever he chose.

Her hands were free. Energy and passion raced together inside her. She tumbled over the first peak, breathless and strong. Now she could touch, now she could enrage him, entice him, weaken him. She moved quickly, demanding when he'd expected surrender. It was too sudden, too frantic to allow him to brace himself against it. Even as she raced to the next peak, she felt the change in him.

He couldn't stop it. She wouldn't permit him to take without giving. His mind swam. Though he tried to clear it, fought to hold himself back, she seduced. Not his body, he'd have given that freely. She seduced his mind until it reeled with her. Emotion raged through him. Clean, hot, strong.

Tangled together, body and mind, they drove each other higher. They took each other over.

Chapter Eight

They were both very careful. Neither Bryan nor Shade wanted to say anything the other could misunderstand. They'd made love, and for each of them it had been more intense, more vital than anything they'd ever experienced. They'd set rules, and for each of them the need to abide by them was paramount.

What had happened between them had left them both more than a little stunned, and more wary than ever.

For a woman like Bryan who was used to saying what she wanted, doing as she pleased, it wasn't easy to walk on eggs twenty-four hours a day. But they'd made themselves clear before making love, she reminded herself. No complications, no commitments. No promises. They'd both failed once at the most important of relationships, marriage. Why should either of them risk failure again?

They traveled in Oklahoma, giving an entire day to a small-town rodeo. Bryan hadn't enjoyed anything as much since the Fourth of July celebrations they'd seen in Kansas. She enjoyed watching the heat of competition, the pitting of man against animal and man against man and the clock. Every man who'd lowered himself onto a bronc or a bull had been determined to make it to the bell.

Some had been young, others had been seasoned, but all had one goal. To win, and then to go on to the next round. She'd liked seeing that a game could be turned into a way of life.

Unable to resist, she bought a pair of boots with fancy stitching and a stubby heel. Since the van was too small to permit indiscriminate souvenir buying, she'd restrained herself this far. But there wasn't any point in being a martyr about it. The boots made her happy, but she resisted buying a leather belt with an oversize silver buckle for Shade. It was just the sort of gesture he might misunderstand. No, they wouldn't give each other flowers or trinkets or pretty words.

She drove south toward Texas while Shade read the paper in the seat beside her. On the radio was a raspy Tina Turner number that was unapologetically sexy.

Summer had reached the point when the heat began to simmer. Bryan didn't need the radio announcer to tell her it was ninety-seven and climbing, but both she and Shade had agreed to use the air-conditioning sparingly on the long trips. On the open highway, the breeze was almost enough. In defense, she was wearing a skimpy tank top and shorts while she drove in her bare feet. She thought of Dallas and an air-conditioned hotel room with cool sheets on a soft mattress.

"I've never been to Texas," she said idly. "I can't imagine any place that has cities fifty and sixty miles across. A cab ride across town could cost you a week's pay."

The paper crackled as he flipped the page. "You live in Dallas or Houston, you own a car."

It was like him to give a brief practical answer and she'd come to accept it. "I'm glad we're taking a couple of days in Dallas to print. Ever spent any time there?"

"A little." He shrugged as he turned the next section of the paper. "Dallas, Houston—those cities are Texas.

Big, sprawling, wealthy. Plenty of Tex-Mex restaurants,
luxury hotels and a freeway system that leaves the out-of-
towner reeling. That's why I routed in San Antonio as
well. It's something apart from the rest of Texas. It's elegant, serene, more European.''

She nodded, glancing out at the road signs. ''Did you
have an assignment in Texas?''

''I tried living in Dallas for a couple of years in between the overseas work.''

It surprised her. She just couldn't picture him anywhere but L.A. ''How'd you like it?''

''Not my style,'' he said simply. ''My ex-wife stayed on
and married oil.''

It was the first time he'd made any sort of reference to
his marriage. Bryan wiped her damp hands on her shorts
and wondered how to handle it. ''You don't mind going
back?''

''No.''

''Does it...'' She trailed off, wondering if she were
getting in deeper than she should.

Shade tossed the paper aside. ''What?''

''Well, does it bother you that she's remarried and
settled? Don't you ever think back and try to figure out
what messed things up?''

''I know what messed things up. There's no use dwell-
ing on it. After you admit you've made a mistake, you've
got to go on.''

''I know.'' She pushed at her sunglasses. ''I just
sometimes wonder why some people can be so happy together, and others so miserable.''

''Some people don't belong with each other.''

''And yet it often seems like they do before they walk
up the aisle.''

''Marriage doesn't work for certain kinds of people.''

Like us? Bryan wondered. After all, they'd both failed at it. Perhaps he was right, and it was as simple as that. "I made a mess out of mine," she commented.

"All by yourself?"

"Seems that way."

"Then you screwed up and married Mr. Perfect."

"Well, I . . ." She glanced over and saw him looking at her, one brow raised and a bland look of anticipation on his face. She'd forgotten he could make her laugh as well as ache. "Mr. Nearly Perfect anyway." She grinned. "I'd have been smarter to look for someone with flaws."

After lighting a cigarette, he rested his feet on the dash as Bryan was prone to do. "Why didn't you?"

"I was too young to realize flaws were easier to deal with. And I loved him." She hadn't realized it would be so painless to say it, to put it in the past tense. "I really did," she murmured. "In a naive, rose-tinted way. At the time I didn't realize I'd have to make a choice between his conception of marriage and my work."

He understood exactly. His wife hadn't been cruel, she hadn't been vindictive. She'd simply wanted things he couldn't give. "So you married Mr. Nearly Perfect and I married Ms. Socially Ambitious. I wanted to take important pictures, and she wanted to join the country club. Nothing wrong with either goal—they just don't mesh."

"But sometimes don't you regret that you couldn't make it fit?"

"Yeah." It came out unexpectedly, surprising him a great deal more than it surprised her. He hadn't realized he had regrets. He hadn't allowed himself to. "You're getting low on gas," he said abruptly. "We'll stop in the next town and fill up."

Bryan had heard of one-horse towns, but nothing fitted the phrase more perfectly than the huddle of houses just over the Oklahoma-Texas border. Everything seemed to be dusty and faded by the heat. Even the buildings looked tired. Perhaps the state was enriched by oil and growth, but this little corner had slept through it.

As a matter of habit, Bryan took her camera as she stepped from the van to stretch her legs. As she walked around the side of the van, the skinny young attendant goggled at her. Shade saw the boy gape and Bryan smile before he walked into the little fan-cooled store behind the pumps.

Bryan found a small, fenced yard just across the street. A woman in a cotton housedress and a faded apron watered the one colorful spot—a splash of pansies along the edge of the house. The grass was yellow, burned by the sun, but the flowers were lush and thriving. Perhaps they were all the woman needed to keep her content. The fence needed painting badly and the screen door to the house had several small holes, but the flowers were a bright, cheerful slash. The woman smiled as she watered them.

Grateful she'd picked up the camera she'd loaded with color film, Bryan tried several angles. She wanted to catch the tired, sun-faded wood of the house and the parched lawn, both a contrast to that bouquet of hope.

Dissatisfied, she shifted again. The light was good, the colors perfect, but the picture was wrong. Why? Stepping back, she took it all in again and asked herself the all-important question. What do I feel?

Then she had it. The woman wasn't necessary, just the illusion of her. Her hand holding the watering can, no more. She could be any woman, anywhere, who needed flowers to complete her home. It was the flowers and the hope they symbolized that were important, and that was what Bryan finally recorded.

Shade came out of the store with a paper bag. He saw Bryan across the street experimenting with angles. Content to wait, he set the bag in the van, drawing out the first cold can before he turned to pay the attendant for the gas. The attendant, Shade noticed, who was so busy watching Bryan he could hardly screw on the gas cap.

"Nice van," he commented, but Shade didn't think he'd even looked at it.

"Thanks." He allowed his own gaze to follow the boy's until it rested on Bryan's. He had to smile. She was a very distracting sight in the swatch of material she called shorts. Those legs, he mused. They seemed to start at the waist and just kept going. Now he knew just how sensitive they could be—on the inside of the knee, just above the ankle, on the warm, smooth skin high on the thigh.

"You and your wife going far?"

"Hmm?" Shade lost track of the attendant as he became just as fascinated by Bryan.

"You and the missus," the boy repeated, sighing a little as he counted out Shade's change. "Going far?"

"Dallas," he murmured. "She's not..." He started to correct the boy's mistake about their relationship, then found himself stopping. The missus. It was a quaint word and somehow appealing. It hardly mattered if a boy in a border town thought Bryan belonged to him. "Thanks," he said absently and, stuffing the change in his pocket, walked to her.

"Good timing," she told him as she crossed toward him. They met in the middle of the road.

"Find something?"

"Flowers." She smiled, forgetting the unmerciful sun. If she breathed deeply enough, she could just smell them over the dust. "Flowers where they didn't belong. I think it's..." She felt the rest of the words slide back down her throat as he reached out and touched her hair.

He never touched her, not in the most casual of ways. Unless they were making love, and then it was never casual. There was never any easy brush of hands, no gentle squeeze. Nothing. Until now in the center of the road between a parched yard and a grimy gas station.

"You're beautiful. Sometimes it stuns me."

What could she say? He never spoke soft words. Now they flowed over her as his fingers trailed to her cheek. His eyes were so dark. She had no idea what he saw when he looked at her, what he felt. She'd never have asked. Perhaps for the first time, he was giving her the opportunity, but she couldn't speak, only stare.

He might have told her that he saw honesty, kindness, strength. He might have told her he felt needs that were growing far beyond the borders he'd set up between him and the rest of the world. If she'd asked, he might have told her that she was making a difference in his life he hadn't foreseen but could no longer prevent.

For the first time he bent toward her and kissed her with an uncharacteristic gentleness. The moment demanded it though he wasn't sure why. The sun was hot and hard, the road dusty, and the smell of gasoline was strong. But the moment demanded tenderness from him. He gave it, surprised that it was in him to offer.

"I'll drive," he murmured as he slipped her hand into his. "It's a long way to Dallas."

His feelings had changed. Not for the city they drove into, but for the woman beside him. Dallas had changed since he'd lived there, but Shade knew from experience that it seemed to change constantly. Even though he'd only lived there briefly, it had seemed as though a new building would grow up overnight. Hotels, office buildings popped up wherever they could find room, and there seemed to be an endless supply of room in Dallas. The architecture leaned toward the futuristic—glass, spirals, pinnacles. But you never had to look far to find that unique southwestern flavor. Men wore cowboy hats as easily as they wore three-piece suits.

They'd agreed on a midtown hotel because it was within walking distance of the darkroom they'd rented for two days. While one worked in the field, the other would have use of the equipment to develop and print. Then they'd switch.

Bryan looked up at the hotel with something like reverence as they pulled up in front of it. Hot running water, feather pillows. Room service. Stepping out, she began to unload her share of the luggage and gear.

"I can't wait," she said as she hauled out another case and felt sweat bead down her back. "I'm going to wallow in the bathtub. I might even sleep there."

Shade pulled out his tripod, then hers. "Do you want your own?"

"My own?" She swung the first camera bag strap over her shoulder.

"Tub."

She looked up and met his calm, questioning glance. He wouldn't assume, she realized, that they'd share a hotel room as they shared the van. They might be lovers, but the lack of strings was still very, very clear. Yes, they'd agreed there'd be no promises but maybe it was time she took the first step. Tilting her head, she smiled.

"That depends."

"On?"

"Whether you agree to wash my back."

He gave her one of his rare, spontaneous smiles as he lifted the rest of the luggage. "Sounds reasonable."

Fifteen minutes later, Bryan dropped her cases inside their hotel room. With equal negligence, she tossed down her shoes. She didn't bother to go to the window and check out the view. There'd be time for that later. There was one vital aspect of the room that demanded immediate attention. She flopped lengthwise on the bed.

"Heaven," she decided and closed her eyes on a sigh. "Absolute heaven."

"Something wrong with your bunk in the van?" Shade stacked his gear in a corner before pulling open the drapes.

"Not a thing. But there's a world of difference between bunk and bed." Rolling onto her back, she stretched across the spread diagonally. "See? It's just not possible to do this on a bunk."

He gave her a mild look as he opened his suitcase. "You won't be able to do that on a bed either when you're sharing it with me."

True enough, she thought as she watched him methodically unpack. She gave her own suitcase an absent glance. It could wait. With the same enthusiasm as she'd had when she'd plopped down, Bryan sprang up. "Hot bath," she said and disappeared into the bathroom.

Shade dropped his shaving kit onto the dresser as he heard the water begin to run. He stopped for a moment, listening. Already, Bryan was beginning to hum. The combination of sounds was oddly intimate—a woman's low voice, the splash of water. Strange that something so simple could make him burn.

Perhaps it'd been a mistake to take only one room in the hotel. It wasn't quite like sharing the van in a campground. Here, they'd had a choice, a chance for privacy and distance. Before the day was over, he mused, her things would be spread around the room, tossed here, flung there. It wasn't like him to freely invite disorder. And yet he had.

Glancing up, he saw himself in the mirror, a dark man with a lean body and a lean face. Eyes a bit too hard, mouth a bit too sensitive. He was too used to his own reflection to wonder what Bryan saw when she looked at him. He saw a man who looked a bit weary and needed a shave. And he didn't want to wonder, though he stared at himself as an artist stares at his subject, if he saw a man who'd already taken one irrevocable step toward change.

Shade looked at his face reflected against the hotel room behind him. Just inside the door were Bryan's cases and the shoes she'd carried into the room. Fleetingly, he wondered if he took his camera and set the shot to take in his reflection, and that of the room and cases behind, just what kind of picture he'd have. He wondered if he'd be able to understand it. Shaking off the mood, he crossed the room and walked into the bath.

Her head moved, but that was all. Though her breath caught when he strolled into the room, Bryan kept her body still and submerged. This kind of intimacy was new and left her vulnerable. Foolishly, she wished she'd poured in a layer of bubbles so that she'd have some mystique.

Shade leaned against the sink and watched her. If she had plans to wash, she was taking her time about it. The little cake of soap sat wrapped in its dish while she lay naked in the tub. It struck him that it was the first time he'd seen her, really seen her in the light. Her body was one long, alluring line. The room was small and steamy.

He wanted her. Shade wondered if a man could die from wanting.

"How's the water?" he asked her.

"Hot." Bryan told herself to relax, be natural. The water that had soothed her now began to arouse.

"Good." Calmly, he began to strip.

Bryan opened her mouth, but shut it again. She'd never seen him undress. Always they'd held to their own unspoken, strict code of ethics. When they camped, each of them changed in the showers. Since they'd become lovers, they'd fallen into a sense of urgency at the end of the day, undressing themselves and each other in the dark van while they made love. Now for the first time she could watch her lover casually reveal his body to her.

She knew how it looked. Her hands had shown her. But it was a far different experience to see the slopes, the contours. Athletic, she thought, in the way of a runner or a hurdler. She supposed it was apt enough. Shade would always expect the next hurdle and be prepared to leap over it.

He left his clothes on the sink but made no comment when he had to step over hers where she'd dropped them.

"You said something about washing your back," he commented as he eased in behind her. Then he swore lightly at the temperature of the water. "You like to take off a couple layers of skin when you bathe?"

She laughed, relaxed and shifted to accommodate him. When his body rubbed and slid against hers, she decided there was something to be said for small tubs. Content, she snuggled back against him, a move that at first surprised him, then pleased.

"We're both a little long," she said as she adjusted her legs. "But it helps that we're on the slim side."

"Keep eating." He gave in to the urge to kiss the top of her head. "It's bound to stick sooner or later."

"Never has." She ran her hand along his thigh, trailing from the knee. It was a light, casual stroke that made his insides churn. "I like to believe I burn up calories just thinking. But you..."

"Me?"

On a quiet sigh, Bryan closed her eyes. He was so complex, so... driven. How could she explain it? She knew so little of what he'd seen and been through. Just one isolated incident, she thought. Just one scar. She didn't have to be told there were others.

"You're very physical," she said at length. "Even your thought pattern has a kind of physical force to it. You don't relax. It's like—" She hesitated for another moment, then plunged. "It's like you're a boxer in the ring. Even between rounds you're tensed and waiting for the bell to ring."

"That's life, isn't it?" But he found himself tracing the line of her neck with his finger. "One long match. A quick breather, then you're up and dancing."

"I've never looked at it that way. It's an adventure," she said slowly. "Sometimes I don't have the energy for it, so I can sit back and watch everyone else go through the moves. Maybe that's why I wanted to be a photographer, so I could pull in little pieces of life and keep them. Think of it, Shade."

Shifting slightly, she turned her head so that she could look at him. "Think of the people we've met, the places we've been and seen. And we're only halfway done. Those rodeo cowboys," she began, eyes brightening. "All they wanted was a plug of tobacco, a bad-tempered horse and a handful of sky. The farmer in Kansas, riding his tractor in the heat of the day, sweating and aching and looking out over acres of his own land. Children playing hopscotch, old men weeding kitchen gardens or playing checkers in the park. That's what life is. It's women with babies on their hips, young girls sunning at the beach and kids splashing in little rubber swimming pools in the side yard.''

He touched her cheek. "Do you believe that?''

Did she? It sounded so simplistic.... Idealistic? She wondered. Frowning, she watched the steam rise from the water. "I believe that you have to take what good there is, what beauty there is, and go with it. The rest has to be dealt with, but not every minute of every day. That woman today...''

Bryan settled back again, not sure why it was so important for her to tell him. "The one in the house just across from where we stopped for gas. Her yard was burning up in the sun, the paint was peeling on the fence. I saw arthritis in her hands. But she was watering her pansies. Maybe she's lived in that tiny little house all her life. Maybe she'll never know what it's like to sit in a new car and smell the leather or fly first class or shop at Saks. But she was watering her pansies. She'd planted, weeded and tended them because they gave her pleasure. Something of value, one bright foolish spot she can look at, smile at. Maybe it's enough.''

"Flowers can't grow everywhere.''

"Yes, they can. You only have to want them to.''

It sounded true when she said it. It sounded like something he'd like to believe. Unconsciously, he rested his cheek against her hair. It was damp from the steam, warm, soft. She made him relax. Just being with her, listening to her, uncurled something in him. But he remembered the rules, those they'd both agreed on. Keep it easy, he reminded himself. Keep it light.

"Do you always have philosophical discussions in the tub?"

Her lips curved. It was so rare and so rewarding to hear that touch of humor in his voice. "I figure if you're going to have one, you might as well be comfortable. Now, about my back..."

Shade picked up the soap and unwrapped it. "Do you want the first shift in the darkroom tomorrow?"

"Mmm." She leaned forward, stretching as he rubbed the dampened soap over her back. Tomorrow was too far away to worry about. "Okay."

"You can have it from eight to twelve."

She started to object to the early hour, then subsided. Some things didn't change. "What're you..." The question trailed off into a sigh as he skimmed the soap around her waist and up to her throat. "I like being pampered."

Her voice was sleepy, but he traced a soapy finger over her nipple and felt the quick shudder. He ran the soap over her in steady circles, lower, still lower, until all thought of relaxation was over. Abruptly, she twisted until he was trapped beneath her, her mouth fixed on his. Her hands raced over him, taking him to the edge before he had a chance to brace himself.

"Bryan—"

"I love to touch you." She slid down until her mouth could skim over his chest, tasting flesh and water. She nibbled, listening to the thunder of his heart, then rubbed her cheek against his damp flesh just to feel, just to experience. She felt him tremble and lie still a moment. When was the last time he'd let himself be made love to? she wondered. Perhaps this time she'd give him no choice.

"Shade." She let her hands roam where they pleased. "Come to bed with me." Before he could answer, she rose. While the water streamed from her, she smiled down at him and slowly pulled the pins from her hair. As it fell, she shook it back, then reached for a towel. It seemed they were through with words.

She waited until he stepped from the tub, then took another towel and rubbed it over him herself. He made no objection, but she could sense him building up the emotional defense. Not this time, she thought. This time it would be different.

As she dried him, she watched his eyes. She couldn't read his thoughts, she couldn't see beneath the desire. For now, it was enough. Taking his hand, she walked toward the bed.

She would love him this time. No matter how strong, how urgent the need, she would show him what he made her feel. Slowly, her arms already around him, she lowered herself to the bed. As the mattress gave, her mouth found his.

The need was no less. It tore through him. But this time, Shade found himself unable to demand, unable to pull her to his pace. She was satiating him with the luxury of being enjoyed. Her lips took him deep, deeper, but lazily. He learned that with her, passion could be built layer by finite layer until there was nothing else. They smelled of the bath they'd shared, of the soap that had rubbed from his skin to hers. She seemed content to breathe it in, to breathe it out while slowly driving him mad.

It was pleasure enough to see him in the late-afternoon sunlight. No darkness now, no shadows. To make love in the light, freely and without barriers was something she hadn't even known she craved. His shoulders were still damp. She could see the sheen of water on them, taste it. When their mouths met she could watch his eyes and see the desire there that echoed what pulsed inside her. In this they were the same, she told herself. In this, if nothing else, they understood each other.

And when he touched her, when she saw his gaze follow the trail of his hand, she trembled. Needs, his and hers, collided, shuddered, then merged together.

There was more here than they'd allowed themselves or each other before. At last this was intimacy, shared knowledge, shared pleasure. No one led, no one held back. For the first time, Shade dropped all pretenses of keeping that thin emotional barrier between them. She filled him, completed him. This time he wanted her—all of her—more than he'd ever wanted anything. He wanted the fun of her, the joy, the kindness. He wanted to believe it could make a difference.

The sun slanted in across the deep, vivid gray of her eyes, highlighting them as he'd once imagined. Her mouth was soft, yielding. Above him her hair flowed down, wild, free. The lowering sun seemed trapped in her skin, making it gleam gold. She might have been something he'd only imagined—woman, lean, agile and primitive—woman without restraints, accepting her own passions. If he photographed her this way, would he recognize her? Would he be able to recapture the emotions she could push into him?

Then she tossed back her head and she was young, vibrant, reachable. This woman he'd know, this feeling he'd recognize if he went away alone for decades. He'd need no photograph to remind him of that one astonishing instant of give and of take.

Shade drew her closer, needing her. You, he thought dizzily as their bodies merged and their thoughts twined. Only you. He watched her eyes slowly close as she gave herself to him.

Chapter Nine

"I could get used to this."

With her camera settled comfortably in her lap, Bryan stretched back in the pirogue, the trim little dugout canoe they'd borrowed from a family who lived in the bayou. A few miles away was the bustling city of Lafayette, Louisiana, but here was a more slumberous view of summer.

Bees humming, shade spreading, birds trilling. Dragonflies. One whisked by too fast for her camera, but slow enough to appreciate. Spanish moss hung overhead, shading and dipping toward the river as the water moved slowly. Why hurry? It was summer, fish were there for catching, flowers were there for picking. Cypress knees thrust their way out of the water and an occasional frog stirred himself enough to plop from his pad and take a swim.

Why hurry indeed? Life was there to be enjoyed.

As Shade had once pointed out, Bryan was adaptable. In the rush of Dallas, she'd worked long hours in the darkroom and on the street. All business. When the moment called for it, she could be efficient, quick and energetic. But here, where the air was heavy and the living slow, she was content to lie back, cross her ankles and wait for whatever came.

"We're supposed to be working," he pointed out.

She smiled. "Aren't we?" While she swung one foot in lazy circles she wished they'd thought to borrow a fishing pole as well. What did it feel like to catch a catfish? "We took dozens of pictures before we got in the boat," she reminded him.

It'd been her idea to detour into the bayou, though she was all but certain Shade had topped her with his pictures of the family who'd welcomed them. She might've charmed them into the use of their boat, but Shade had won hands down with camera work.

"The one you took of Mrs. Bienville shelling beans has to be fabulous. Her hands." Bryan shook her head and relaxed. "I've never seen such hands on a woman. I imagine she could make the most elegant of soufflés right before she went out and cut down a tree."

"Cajuns have their own way of life, their own rules."

She tilted her head as she studied him. "You like that."

"Yeah." He rowed not because they needed to get anywhere but because it felt so good. It warmed his muscles and relaxed his mind. He nearly smiled thinking that being with Bryan accomplished almost the same thing. "I like the independence and the fact that it works."

Bryan lay back listening to the buzz and hum of insects, sounds of the river. They'd walked along another river in San Antonio, but the sounds had been different there. Soft Spanish music from musicians, the clink of silver on china from the outdoor cafés. It had been fabulous at night, she remembered. The lights had glowed on the water, the water had rippled from the river taxis, the taxis had been full of people content with the Texas version of a gondola. She'd taken a picture of two young lovers, newlyweds perhaps, huddled together on one of the arched stone bridges above the water.

When they'd driven into Galveston she'd seen yet another kind of Texas, one with white sand beaches, ferries and bicycle surreys. It'd been easier to talk Shade into renting one than she'd imagined. With a smile, she thought of just how far they'd come, not only in miles. They were working together, and when he could be distracted, they played.

In Malibu, they'd gone their separate ways on the beach. In Galveston, after two hours of work, they'd walked hand in hand along the shore. A small thing for many people, Bryan mused, but not for either of them.

Each time they made love, there seemed to be something more. She didn't know what it was, but she didn't question it. It was Shade she wanted to be with, laugh with, talk with. Every day she discovered something new, something different about the country and the people. She discovered it with Shade. Perhaps that was all the answer she needed.

What was it about him? Whether she chose to or not, there were times she wondered. What was it about Shade Colby that made her happy? He wasn't always patient. One moment he might be generous and something close to sweet, and the next he could be as cool and aloof as a stranger. Being with him wasn't without its frustrations for a woman accustomed to less fluctuating moods. But being with him was exactly what she wanted.

At the moment, he was relaxed. He wasn't often, she knew, but the mood of the river seemed to have seeped into him. Still, he was watching. Someone else might have floated down the river, glancing at the scenery, appreciating the overall effect. Shade dissected it.

This she understood because it was her way as well. A tree might be studied for the texture of its leaves, the grain in the wood, the pattern of shade and light it allowed to fall on the ground. A layman might take a perfectly competent picture of the tree, but it would be only that. When Bryan took the picture, she wanted it to pull feelings out of the viewer.

She specialized in people, Bryan remembered as she watched Shade draw the oars through the water. Landscapes, still lifes, she considered a change of pace. It was the human element that had and would always fascinate her. If she wanted to understand her feelings about Shade, maybe it was time to treat him as she would any other subject.

Under half-lowered lashes, she studied and dissected. He had very dominating physical looks, she mused. Being dominated was definitely not her ambition in life. Perhaps that was why she was so often drawn to his mouth, because it was sensitive, vulnerable.

She knew his image—cool, distant, pragmatic. Part of it was true, she thought, but part of it was illusion. Once she'd thought to photograph him in shadows. Now she wondered what sort of study she'd get if she photographed him in quiet sunlight. Without giving herself a chance to think, she lifted her camera, framed him in and shot.

"Just testing," she said lightly when he arched a brow. "And after all, you've already taken a couple of me."

"So I have." He remembered the picture he'd taken of her brushing her hair on the rock in Arizona. He hadn't told her that he'd sent the print back to the magazine, nor did he doubt it would be used in the final essay. Nor had he told her it was a print he intended to keep in his private collection.

"Hold it a minute." With brisk, professional movements, she changed her lens, adjusted for distance and depth and focused on a heron perched on top of a cypress knee. "A place like this," she murmured as she took two more insurance shots, "makes you think summer just goes on and on."

"Maybe we should take another three months traveling back and do autumn."

"It's tempting." She stretched back again. "Very tempting. A study on all seasons."

"Your clients might get testy."

"Unfortunately true. Still..." She let her fingers dip into the water. "We miss the seasons in L.A. I'd like to see spring in Virginia and winter in Montana." Tossing her braid back, she sat up. "Have you ever thought of chucking it, Shade? Just packing up and moving to, oh, say Nebraska, and setting up a little studio. Wedding and graduation pictures, you know."

He gave her a long steady look. "No."

With a laugh, she flopped back. "Me either."

"You wouldn't find many megastars in Nebraska."

She narrowed her eyes but spoke mildly. "Is that another subtle shot at my work?"

"Your work," he began as he gently turned the boat back, "is uniformly excellent. Otherwise, we wouldn't be working together."

"Thank you very much. I think."

"And because of the quality of your work," he continued, "I wonder why you limit yourself to the pretty people."

"It's my specialty." She saw a clump of wild flowers on the mossy, muddy edge of the river. Carefully she adjusted her camera again. "And a great many of my subjects are far from pretty—physically or emotionally. They interest me," she said before he could comment. "I like to find out what's under the image and give a glimpse of it."

And she was well skilled at it, he decided. In truth, he'd discovered he admired her for it—not only for her skill, but for her perception. He simply couldn't rationalize her following the glitz trail. "Culture art?"

If he'd meant it as an insult, however mild, it missed its mark. "Yes. And if you asked, I'a say Shakespeare wrote culture art. Are you hungry?"

"No." Fascinating woman, he thought, as reluctant as ever to be fascinated. He craved her, it was true. Her body, her company. But he couldn't resolve the constant fascination she held for him, mind to mind. "You had a bowl of shrimp and rice big enough to feed a family of four before we started out."

"That was hours ago."

"Two to be exact."

"Picky," she mumbled and stared up at the sky. So peaceful, she mused. So simple. Moments like this were meant to be savored. Lowering her gaze she smiled at him. "Ever made love in a pirogue?"

He had to grin. She made it impossible to do otherwise. "No, but I don't think we should ever refuse a new experience."

Bryan touched her tongue to her top lip. "Come here."

They left the lazy, insect-humming air of the bayou behind and landed in bustling, raucous New Orleans. Sweating trumpet players on Bourbon Street, merchants fanning themselves in the Farmers' Market, artists and tourists around Jackson Square—it was a taste of the south, they both agreed, that was as far apart from the South as San Antonio had been apart from Texas.

From there, they traveled north to Mississippi for a touch of July in the deep south. Heat and humidity. Tall, cool drinks and precious shade. Life was different here.

In the cities, men sweated in white shirts and loosened ties. In the rural districts, farmers worked under the sweltering sun. But they moved more slowly than their counterparts to the north and west. Perhaps temperatures soaring to a hundred and more caused it, or perhaps it was just a way of life.

Children exercised the privilege of youth and wore next to nothing. Their bodies were browned and damp and dusty. In a city park, Bryan took a close-up of a grinning boy with mahogany skin cooling himself in a fountain.

The camera hadn't intimidated him. As she homed in, he'd laughed at her, squealing as the water cascaded over him, white and cool until he'd looked encased in glass.

In a small town just northwest of Jackson, they stumbled across a Little League game. It wasn't much of a field, and the bleachers looked as if they'd object to more than fifty people at a time, but they pulled off and parked between a pickup and a rusted-out sedan.

"This is great." Bryan grabbed her camera bag.

"You just smell hot dogs."

"That too," she agreed easily. "But this *is* summer. We might get to a Yankee game in New York, but we'll get better pictures here today." She hooked her arm through his before he could get too far away. "I'll reserve judgment on the hot dogs."

Shade took a long, sweeping view. The crowd was spread out, on the grass, in folding chairs, on the bleachers. They cheered, complained, gossiped and gulped iced drinks. He was all but certain everyone there knew one another by name or by sight. He watched an old man in a baseball cap casually spit out a plug of tobacco before he berated the umpire.

"I'm going to wander around a bit," he decided, considering a seat on the bleachers too limiting for the moment.

"Okay." Bryan had taken her own scan and considered the bleachers the focal point for what she wanted.

They separated, Shade moving toward the old man who'd already captured his attention. Bryan walked to the bleachers where she and the onlookers would have a solid view of the game.

The players wore white pants, already grass stained and dusty, with bright red or blue shirts emblazoned with team names. A good many of them were too small for the uniforms and the mitts looked enormous on the ends of gangling arms. Some wore spikes, some wore sneakers. A few had batting gloves hung professionally from their back pocket.

It was the hats, she decided, that told of the individual's personality. One might wear it snug or tipped back, another tilted rakishly over the eyes. She wanted an action shot, something that would bring the color and the personalities together with the sport itself. Until something formed for her, Bryan contented herself with taking a shot of the second baseman, who passed the time until the batter stepped into the box by kicking his spikes against the bag and blowing bubbles with his wad of gum.

Scooting up another step, she tried her long lens. Better, she decided, and was pleased to see that her second baseman had a face full of freckles. Above her, someone snapped gum and whistled when the umpire called a strike.

Bryan lowered her camera and allowed herself to become involved in the game. If she wanted to portray the atmosphere, she had to let herself feel it. It was more than the game, she thought, it was the feeling of community. As the batters came up, people in the crowd called them by name, tossing out casual remarks that indicated a personal knowledge. But the sides were definitely drawn.

Parents had come to the game from work, grandparents had pushed away from an early dinner and neighbors had chosen the game against an evening by the TV. They had their favorites, and they weren't shy about rooting for them.

The next batter interested Bryan mainly because she was a strikingly pretty girl of about twelve. At a glance, Bryan would've set her more easily at a ballet bar than home plate. But when she watched the way the girl gripped the bat and bent into her stance, Bryan lifted her camera. This was one to watch.

Bryan caught her in the first swing on a strike. Though the crowd moaned, Bryan was thrilled with the flow of movement. She might be shooting a Little League game in a half-forgotten town in Mississippi, but she thought of her studio work with the prima ballerina. The batter poised for the pitch, and Bryan poised for the next shot. She had to wait, growing impatient, through two balls.

"Low and outside," she heard someone mumble beside her. All she could think was if the girl walked she'd lose the picture she wanted.

Then it came over, too fast for Bryan to judge the placement of the ball, but the girl connected with a solid swing. The batter took off, and using the motor drive, Bryan followed her around the bases. When she rounded second, Bryan homed in on her face. Yes, Maria would understand that look, Bryan thought. Strain, determination and just plain guts. Bryan had her as she slid into third with a storm of dust and a swing of body.

"Wonderful!" She lowered the camera, so thrilled that she didn't even realize she'd spoken out loud. "Just wonderful!"

"That's our girl."

Distracted, Bryan glanced over to the couple beside her. The woman was her own age, perhaps a year or two older. She was beaming. The man beside her was grinning over a wad of gum.

Perhaps she hadn't heard properly. They were so young. "She's your daughter?"

"Our oldest." The woman slipped a hand into her husband's. Bryan saw the plain twin wedding bands. "We've got three others running around here, but they're more interested in the concession stand than the game."

"Not our Carey." The father looked out to where his daughter took a short lead on third. "She's all business."

"I hope you don't mind my taking her picture."

"No." The woman smiled again. "Do you live in town?"

It was a polite way to find out who she was. Bryan hadn't a doubt the woman knew everyone within ten miles. "No, I'm traveling." She paused as the next batter blooped to right field and brought Carey home. "Actually, I'm a free-lance photographer on assignment for *Life-style*. Perhaps you've heard of it."

"Sure." The man jerked a head at his wife as he kept his eyes on the game. "She picks it up every month."

Pulling a release form out of her bag, she explained her interest in using Carey's picture. Though she kept it short and her voice low, word spread throughout the bleachers. Bryan found herself answering questions and dealing with curiosity. In order to handle it all in the simplest fashion, she climbed down from the bleachers, changed to a wide angle lens and took a group shot. Not a bad study, she decided, but she didn't want to spend the next hour having people pose for her. To give the baseball fans time to shift their attention back to the game, she wandered to the concession stand.

"Any luck?"

She swiveled her head around to see Shade fall into step beside her. "Yeah. You?"

He nodded, then leaned on the counter of the stand. There was no relief from the heat though the sun was lowering. It promised to be as sweltering a night as it had a day. He ordered two large drinks and two hot dogs.

"Know what I'd love?" she asked as she began to bury her hot dog under relish.

"A shovel?"

Ignoring him, she piled on mustard. "A long, cool dip in an enormous pool, followed closely by an iced margarita."

"For now you'll have to settle for the driver's seat of the van. It's your turn."

She shrugged. A job was a job. "Did you see the girl who hit the triple?" They walked over the uneven grass toward the van.

"Kid that ran like a bullet?"

"Yes. I sat next to her parents in the stands. They have four kids."

"So?"

"Four kids," she repeated. "And I'd swear she wasn't more than thirty. How do people do it?"

"Ask me later and I'll show you."

With a laugh, she jabbed him with her elbow. "That's not what I meant—though I like the idea. What I mean is, here's this couple—young, attractive. You could tell they even liked each other."

"Amazing."

"Don't be cynical," she ordered as she pulled open the door to the van. "A great many couples don't, especially when they've got four kids, a mortgage and ten or twelve years of marriage under their belts."

"Now who's being cynical?"

She started to speak and frowned instead. "I guess I am," she mused as she turned on the engine. "Maybe I've picked a world that's tilted my outlook, but when I see a happily married couple with a track record, I'm impressed."

"It is impressive." Carefully, he stored his camera bag under the dash before he sat back. "When it really works."

"Yeah."

She fell silent, remembering the jolt of envy and longing she'd felt when she'd framed the Browns in her viewfinder. Now, weeks and miles later, it was another jolt for Bryan to realize she hadn't brushed off that peculiar feeling. She had managed to put it aside, somewhere to the back of her mind, but it popped out again now as she thought of the couple in the bleachers of a small-town park.

Family, cohesion. Bonding. Did some people just keep promises better than others? she wondered. Or were some people simply unable to blend their lives with someone else's, make those adjustments, the compromises?

When she looked back, she believed both she and Rob had tried, but in their own ways. There'd been no meeting of the minds, but two separate thought patterns making decisions that never melded with the other's. Did that mean that a successful marriage depended on the mating of two people who thought along the same lines?

With a sigh, she turned onto the highway that would lead them into Tennessee. If it were true, she decided, she was much better off single. Though she'd met a great many people she liked and could have fun with, she'd never met anyone who thought the way she did. Especially the man seated next to her with his nose already buried in the newspaper. There alone they were radically different.

He'd read that paper and every paper in every town they stopped in from cover to cover, devouring the words. She'd skim the headlines, glance over the style or society pages and go straight for the comics. If she wanted news, she'd rather have it in spurts on the radio or blurbs on televisions. Reading was for relaxation, and relaxation was not an analysis of détente.

Relationships. She thought back on the discussion she'd had with Lee just weeks before. No, she simply wasn't cut out for relationships on a long-term basis. Shade himself had pointed out that some people just weren't capable of permanency. She'd agreed, hadn't she? Why should the truth suddenly depress her?

Whatever her feelings were for Shade, and she'd yet to define them satisfactorily, she wasn't going to start smelling orange blossoms. Maybe she had a few twinges when she saw couples together who seemed to complete each other rather than compete, but that was only natural. After all, she didn't want to start making adjustments in her life-style to accommodate someone else at this stage. She was perfectly content the way things were.

If she were in love... Bryan felt the twinge again and ignored it. *If* she were, it would complicate things. The fact was she was very happy with a successful career, her freedom and an attractive, interesting lover. She'd be crazy if she wasn't happy. She'd be insane to change one single thing.

"And it doesn't have anything to do with being afraid," she said aloud.

"What?"

She turned to Shade and, to his astonishment and hers, blushed. "Nothing," she muttered. "Thinking out loud."

He gave her a long quiet look. Her expression came very close to a baffled sort of pout. Giving in to the urge, he leaned over and touched a hand to her cheek. "You're not eating your hot dog."

She could have wept. For some absurd reason, she wanted to stop the van, drop her head on the steering wheel and drown herself in hot, violent tears. "Not hungry," she managed.

"Bryan." He watched her snatch her sunglasses from the dash and push them on though the sun was riding low. "Are you all right?"

"Fine." She took a deep breath and kept her eyes straight ahead. "I'm fine."

No, she wasn't. Though strain in her voice was rare, he recognized it. Only a few weeks before, he'd have shrugged and turned back to his reading. Deliberately, he dropped the paper on the floor at his feet. "What is it?"

"Nothing." She cursed herself and turned up the radio. Shade simply switched it off.

"Pull over."

"What for?"

"Just pull over."

With more violence than necessary, Bryan swung the van toward the shoulder, slowed and stopped. "We won't make very good time if we stop ten minutes after we start."

"We won't be making any time at all until you tell me what's wrong."

"Nothing's wrong!" Then she gritted her teeth and sat back. It wasn't any use saying nothing was wrong if you snarled at the same time. "I don't know," she evaded. "I'm edgy, that's all."

"You?"

She turned on him with a vengeance. "I've a right to foul moods, Colby. You don't have a patent on them."

"You certainly have," he said mildly. "Since it's the first one I've witnessed, I'm interested."

"Don't be so damn patronizing."

"Wanna fight?"

She stared through the windshield. "Maybe."

"Okay." Willing to oblige, he made himself comfortable. "About anything in particular?"

She swung her head around, ready to pounce on anything. "Do you have to bury your face in a paper every time I get behind the wheel?"

He smiled maddeningly. "Yes, dear."

A low sound came from her throat as she stared through the windshield again. "Never mind."

"I could point out that you have a habit of falling asleep when you sit in this seat."

"I said never mind." She reached for the key. "Just never mind. You make me sound like a fool."

He put his hand over hers before she could turn the key. "You sound foolish skirting around whatever's bothering you." He wanted to reach her. Without being aware when, he'd passed the point where he could tell himself not to get involved and follow the advice. Whether he wanted it or not, whether she accepted it or not, he was involved. Slowly, he lifted her hand to his lips. "Bryan, I care."

She sat there stunned that a simple statement could spin through her with such force. *I care*. He'd used the same phrase when he'd spoken about the woman who'd caused his nightmare. Along with the pleasure his words brought her came an inescapable sense of responsibility. He wouldn't allow himself to care indiscriminately. Glancing up, she met his eyes, patient, puzzled, as they studied her face.

"I care too," she said quietly. She twined her fingers with his, only briefly, but it unsettled them both.

Shade took the next step carefully, not certain of her, or himself. "Is that what's bothering you?"

She let out a long breath, as wary as he now. "Some. I'm not used to it . . . not like this."

"Neither am I."

She nodded, watching the cars breeze by. "I guess we'd both better take it easy then."

"Sounds logical." And next to impossible, he thought. Right now he wanted to gather her close, forget where they were. Just hold her, he realized. It was all he wanted to do. With an effort, he drew back. "No complications?"

She managed to smile. Rule number one was the most important, after all. "No complications," she agreed. Again she reached for the key. "Read your paper, Colby," she said lightly. "I'll drive until dark."

Chapter Ten

They took a slice out of Tennessee—Nashville, Chattanooga, caught the eastern corner of Arkansas—mountains and legends, and headed up through Twain's Missouri to Kentucky. There they found tobacco leaves, mountain laurel, Fort Knox and Mammoth Cave, but when Bryan thought of Kentucky, she thought of horses. Kentucky was sleek, glossy Thoroughbreds grazing on rich grass. It made her think of long-legged foals running in wide pastures and wide-chested colts pounding the track at Churchill Downs.

As they crossed the state toward Louisville, she saw much more. Tidy suburban homes bordered the larger cities and smaller towns as they did in every state across the country. Farms spread acre after acre—tobacco, horses, grain. Cities rose with their busy office buildings and harried streets. So much was the same as it had been to the west and to the south and yet so much was different.

"Daniel Boone and the Cherokees," Bryan murmured as they traveled down another long, monotonous highway.

"What?" Slade glanced up from the map he'd been checking. When Bryan was driving, it didn't hurt to keep an eye on the navigation.

"Daniel Boone and the Cherokees," Bryan repeated. She increased the speed to pass a camper loaded down with bikes on the back bumper and fishing poles on the front. And where were they going? she wondered. Where had they come from? "I was thinking maybe it's the history of a place that makes it different from another. Maybe it's the climate, the topography."

Shade glanced back down at the map, idly figuring the time and mileage. He didn't give the camper rolling along behind them more than a passing thought. "Yes."

Bryan shot him an exasperated smile. One and one always added up to two for Shade. "But people are basically the same, don't you think? I imagine if you took a cross section of the country and polled, you'd find out that most people want the same things. A roof over their heads, a good job, a couple weeks off a year to play."

"Flowers in the garden?"

"All right, yes." She gave a careless little shrug and refused to believe it sounded foolish. "I think most peoples' wants are fairly simple. Italian shoes and a trip to Barbados might add in, but it's the basic things that touch everyone. Healthy children, a nest egg, a steak on the grill."

"You've a way of simplifying things, Bryan."

"Maybe, but I don't see any reason to complicate them."

Interested, he set down the map and turned to her. Perhaps he'd avoided digging too deeply into her, leery of what he might find. But now, behind his sunglasses, his eyes were direct. So was his question. "What do you want?"

"I..." She faltered a moment, frowning as she took the van around a long curve. "I don't know what you mean."

He thought she did, but they always seemed to end up fencing. "A roof over your head, a good job? Are those the most important things to you?"

Two months before she might've shrugged and agreed. Her job came first and gave her whatever she needed. That was the way she'd planned it, the way she'd wanted it. She wasn't sure any longer. Since she'd left L.A., she'd seen too much, felt too much. "I have those things," she said evasively. "Of course I want them."

"And?"

Uncomfortable, she shifted. She hadn't meant to have her idle speculation turned back on her. "I wouldn't turn down a trip to Barbados."

He didn't smile as she'd hoped he would, but continued to watch her from behind the protection of tinted glasses. "You're still simplifying."

"I'm a simple person."

Her hands were light and competent on the wheel, her hair scooped back in its habitual braid. She wore no makeup, a pair of faded cut-offs and a T-shirt two sizes too large for her. "No," he decided after a moment, "you're not. You only pretend to be."

Abruptly wary, she shook her head. Since her outburst in Mississippi, Bryan had managed to keep herself level, and to keep herself, she admitted, from thinking too deeply. "You're a complicated person, Shade, and you see complications where there aren't any."

She wished she could see his eyes. She wished she could see the thoughts behind them.

"I know what I see when I look at you, and it isn't simple."

She shrugged carelessly, but her body had begun to tense. "I'm easily read."

He corrected her with a short, concise word calmly spoken. Bryan blinked once, then gave her attention to the road. "Well, I'm certainly not full of mysteries."

Wasn't she? Shade watched the thin gold loops sway at her ears. "I wonder what you're thinking when you lie beside me after we've made love—in those minutes after passion and before sleep. I often wonder."

She wondered, too. "After we've made love," she said in a tolerably steady voice, "I have a hard time thinking at all."

This time he did smile. "You're always soft and sleepy," he murmured, making her tremble. "And I wonder what you might say, what I might hear if you spoke your thoughts aloud."

That I might be falling in love with you. That every day we have together takes us a day closer to the end. That I can't imagine what my life will be like when I don't have you there to touch, to talk to. Those were her thoughts, but she said nothing.

She had her secrets, Shade thought. Just as he did. "One day, before we're finished, you'll tell me."

He was easing her into a corner; Bryan felt it but she didn't know why. "Haven't I told you enough already?"

"No." Giving in to the urge that came over him more and more often, he touched her cheek. "Not nearly."

She tried to smile, but she had to clear her throat to speak. "This is a dangerous conversation to have when I'm driving on an interstate at sixty miles an hour."

"It's a dangerous conversation in any case." Slowly, he drew his hand away. "I want you, Bryan. I can't look at you and not want you."

She fell silent, not because he was saying things she didn't want to hear, but because she no longer knew how to deal with them, and with him. If she spoke, she might say too much and break whatever bond had begun to form. She couldn't tell him so, but it was a bond she wanted.

He waited for her to speak, needing her to say something after he'd all but crossed over the line they'd drawn in the beginning. Risk. He'd taken one. Couldn't she see it? Needs. He needed her. Couldn't she feel it? But she remained silent, and the step forward became a step back.

"Your exit's coming up," he told her. Picking up the map, he folded it carefully. Bryan switched lanes, slowed down and left the highway.

Kentucky had made her think of horses; horses led them to Louisville, and Louisville to Churchill Downs. The Derby was long over, but there were races and there were crowds. If they were going to include in their glimpse of summer those who spent an afternoon watching races and betting, where else would they go?

The moment Bryan saw it she thought of a dozen angles. There were cathedral-like domes and clean white buildings that gave a quiet elegance to the frenzy. The track was the focal point, a long oval of packed dirt. Stands rose around it. Bryan walked about, wondering just what kind of person would come there, or to any track, to plop down two dollars—or two hundred—on a race that would take only minutes. Again, she saw the variety.

There was the man with reddened arms and a sweaty T-shirt who pored over a racing form, and another in casually elegant slacks who sipped something long and cool. She saw women in quietly expensive dresses holding field glasses and families treating their children to the sport of kings. There was a man in a gray hat with tattoos snaking up both arms and a boy laughing on top of his father's shoulders.

They'd been to baseball games, tennis matches, drag races across the country. Always she saw faces in the crowd that seemed to have nothing in common except the game. The games had been invented, Bryan mused, and turned into industries. It was an interesting aspect of human nature. But people kept the games alive; they wanted to be amused, they wanted to compete.

She spotted one man leaning against the rail watching a race as though his life depended on the outcome. His body was coiled, his face damp. She caught him in profile.

A quick scan showed her a woman in a pale rose dress and summer hat. She watched the race idly, distanced from it the way an empress might've been from a contest in a coliseum. Bryan framed her as the crowd roared the horses down the stretch.

Shade rested a hip on the rail and shot the horses in varying positions around the track, ending with the final lunge across the finish line. Before, he'd framed in the odds board where numbers flashed and tempted. Now he waited until the results were posted and focused on it again.

Before the races were over, Shade saw Bryan standing at the two-dollar window. With her camera hanging around her neck and her ticket in her hand, she walked back toward the stands.

"Haven't you got any willpower?" he asked her.

"No." She'd found a vending machine and offered Shade a candy bar that was already softening in the heat. "Besides, there's a horse in the next race called Made in the Shade." When his eyebrow lifted up, she grinned. "How could I resist?"

He wanted to tell her she was foolish. He wanted to tell her she was unbearably sweet. Instead, he drew her sunglasses down her nose until he could see her eyes. "What's his number?"

"Seven."

Shade glanced over at the odds board and shook his head. "Thirty-five to one. How'd you bet?"

"To win, of course."

Taking her arm, he led her down to the rail again. "You can kiss your two bucks goodbye, hotshot."

"Or I can win seventy." Bryan pushed her glasses back in place. "Then I'll take you out to dinner. If I lose," she continued as the horses were led to the starting gate, "I've always got plastic. I can still take you out to dinner."

"Deal," Shade told her as the bell rang.

Bryan watched the horses lunge forward. They were nearly to the first turn before she managed to find number seven third from the back. She glanced up to see Shade shake his head.

"Don't give up on him yet."

"When you bet on a long shot, love, you've got to be ready to lose."

A bit flustered by his absent use of the endearment, she turned back to the race. Shade rarely called her by name, much less one of those sweetly intimate terms. A long shot, she agreed silently. But she wasn't altogether sure she was as prepared to lose as she might've been.

"He's moving up," she said quickly as number seven passed three horses with long, hard-driving strides. Forgetting herself, she leaned on the rail and laughed. "Look at him! He's moving up." Lifting her camera, she used the telephoto lens like a field glass. "God, he's beautiful," she murmured. "I didn't know he was so beautiful."

Watching the horse, she forgot the race, the competition. He was beautiful. She could see the jockey riding low in a blur of color that had a style of its own, but it was the horse, muscles bunching, legs pounding, that held her fascinated. He wanted to win; she could feel it. No matter how many races he'd lost, how many times he'd been led back to the stables sweating, he wanted to win.

Hope. She sensed it but she no longer heard the call of the crowd around her. The horse straining to overtake the leaders hadn't lost hope. He believed he could win, and if you believed hard enough... With a last burst of speed, he nipped by the leader and crossed the wire like a champion.

"I'll be damned," Shade murmured. He found he had his arm around Bryan's shoulders as they watched the winner take his victory lap in long, steady strides.

"Beautiful." Her voice was low and thick.

"Hey." Shade tipped up her chin when he heard the tears. "It was only a two-dollar bet."

She shook her head. "He did it. He wanted to win and he just didn't give up until he did."

Shade ran a finger down her nose. "Ever hear of luck?"

"Yeah." More composed, she took his hand in hers. "And this had nothing to do with it."

For a moment he studied her, then with a shake of his head he lowered his mouth to hers lightly, sweetly. "And this from a woman who claims to be simple."

And happy, she thought as her fingers laced with his. Ridiculously happy. "Let's go collect my winnings."

"There was a rumor," he began as they worked their way through the stands, "about you buying dinner."

"Yeah. I heard something about it myself."

She was a woman of her word. That evening as the sky flashed with lightning and echoed with the thunder of a summer storm, they stepped into a quiet, low-lighted restaurant.

"Linen napkins," Bryan murmured to Shade as they were led to a table.

He laughed in her ear as he pulled out her chair. "You're easily impressed."

"True enough," she agreed, "but I haven't seen a linen napkin since June." Picking it off her plate, she ran it through her hands. It was smooth and rich. "There isn't a vinyl seat or a plastic light in this place. There won't be any little plastic containers of ketchup either." With a wink, she knocked a finger against a plate and let it ring. "Try that with paper and all you get is a thump."

Shade watched her experiment with the water glass next. "All this from the queen of fast food?"

"A steady diet of hamburgers is all right, but I like a change of pace. Let's have champagne," she decided as their waiter came over. She glanced at the list, made her choice and turned back to Shade again.

"You just blew your winnings on a bottle of wine."

"Easy come, easy go." Cupping her chin on her hands, she smiled at him. "Did I mention you look wonderful by candlelight?"

"No." Amused, he leaned forward as well. "Shouldn't that be my line?"

"Maybe, but you didn't seem in a rush to come out with it. Besides, I'm buying. However..." She sent him a slow, simmering look. "If you'd like to say something flattering I wouldn't be offended."

Lazily, she ran a finger along the back of his hand, making him wonder why any man would object to the benefits of women's liberation. It wasn't a hardship to be wined and dined. Nor would it be a hardship to relax and be seduced. All the same, Shade decided as he lifted her hand to his lips, there was something to be said for partnership.

"I might say that you always look lovely, but tonight..." He let his gaze wander over her face. "Tonight, you take my breath away."

Momentarily flustered, she allowed her hand to stay in his. How was it he could say such things so calmly, so unexpectedly? And how could she, when she was used to casual, inconsequential compliments from men, deal with one that seemed so serious? Carefully, she warned herself. Very carefully.

"In that case I'll have to remember to use lipstick more often."

With a quick smile he kissed her fingers again. "You forgot to put any on."

"Oh." Stuck, Bryan stared at him.

"Madam?" The wine steward held out the bottle of champagne, label up.

"Yes." She let out a quiet breath. "Yes, that's fine."

Still watching Shade, she heard the cork give into pressure and the wine bubble into her glass. She sipped, closing her eyes to enjoy it. Then with a nod she waited until the steward filled both glasses. Steadier, Bryan lifted her glass and smiled at Shade.

"To?"

"One summer," he said and touched his rim to hers. "One fascinating summer."

It made her lips curve again, so that her eyes reflected the smile as she sipped. "I expected you to be a terrible bore to work with."

"Really." Shade let the champagne rest on his tongue a moment. Like Bryan, it was smooth and quiet with energy bubbling underneath. "I expected you to be a pain in the—"

"However," she interrupted dryly. "I've been pleased that my preconception didn't hold true." She waited a moment. "And yours?"

"Did," he said easily, then laughed when she narrowed her eyes at him. "But I wouldn't have enjoyed you nearly as much if it'd been otherwise."

"I liked your other compliment better," she mumbled and picked up her menu. "But I suppose since you're stingy with them, I have to take what I get."

"I only say what I mean."

"I know." She pushed back her hair as she skimmed the menu. "But I—oh look, they've got chocolate mousse."

"Most people start at the appetizers."

"I'd rather work backward, then I can gauge how much I want to eat and still have room for dessert."

"I can't imagine you turning down anything chocolate."

"Right you are."

"What I can't understand is how you can shovel it in the way you do and not be fat."

"Just lucky, I guess." With the menu open over her plate she smiled at him. "Don't you have any weaknesses, Shade?"

"Yeah." He looked at her until she was baffled and flustered again. "A few." And one of them, he thought as he watched her eyes, was becoming more and more acute.

"Are you ready to order?"

Distracted, Bryan looked up at the well-mannered waiter. "What?"

"Are you ready to order?" he repeated. "Or would you like more time?"

"The lady'll have the chocolate mousse," Shade said smoothly.

"Yes, sir." Unflappable, the waiter marked it down. "Will that be all?"

"Not by a long shot," Shade told him and picked up his wine again.

With a laugh, Bryan worked her way through the menu.

"Stuffed." Bryan decided over an hour later as they drove through a hard, driving rain. "Absolutely stuffed."

Shade cruised through an amber light. "Watching you eat is an amazing way to pass the time."

"We're here to entertain," she said lightly. Snuggled back in her seat with champagne swimming in her head and thunder grumbling in a bad-tempered sky, she was content to ride along wherever he chose to go. "It was sweet of you to let me have a bite of your cheesecake."

"Half," Shade corrected her. Deliberately he turned away from the campground they'd decided on that afternoon. The wipers made quick swishing sounds against the windshield. "But you're welcome."

"It was lovely." She let out a sigh, quiet and sleepy. "I like being pampered. Tonight should get me through another month of fast-food chains and diners with stale doughnuts." Content, she glanced around at the dark, wet streets, the puddles at the curbs. She liked the rain, especially at night when it made everything glisten. Watching it, she fell to dreaming, rousing herself only when he turned into the lot of a small motel.

"No campground tonight," he said before she could question. "Wait here while I get a room."

She didn't have time to comment before he was out of the van and dashing through the rain. No campground, she thought, looking over her shoulder at the narrow twin bunks on either side of the van. No skinny, makeshift beds and trickling showers.

With a grin, she jumped up and began to gather his equipment and hers. She never gave the suitcases a thought.

"Champagne, linen napkins and now a bed," She laughed as he climbed back into the van, soaking wet. "I'm going to get spoiled."

He wanted to spoil her. There was no logic to it, only fact. Tonight, if only for tonight, he wanted to spoil her. "Room's around the back." When Bryan dragged the equipment forward, he drove slowly around, checking numbers on the lines of doors. "Here." He strapped camera bags over his shoulder. "Wait a minute." She'd grabbed another bag and her purse by the time he'd pulled open her door from the outside. To her astonishment, she found herself lifted into his arms.

"Shade!" But the rain slapped into her face, making her gasp as he dashed across the lot to an outside door.

"Least I could do after you sprang for dinner," he told her as he maneuvered the oversize key into the lock. Bryan was laughing as he struggled to open the door holding her, the camera bags and tripods.

Kicking the door closed with his foot, he fastened his mouth on hers. Still laughing, Bryan clung to him.

"Now we're both wet," she murmured, running a hand through his hair.

"We'll dry off in bed." Before she knew his intention, Bryan was falling through the air and landing with two bounces full length onto the mattress.

"So romantic," she said dryly, but her body stayed limp. She lay there, smiling, because he'd made a rare frivolous gesture and she intended to enjoy it.

Her dress clung to her, her hair fanned out. He'd seen her change for dinner and knew she wore a thin teddy cut high at the thigh, low over her breasts, and sheer, sheer stockings. He could love her now, love her for hours. It wouldn't be enough. He knew how relaxed, how pliant her body could be. How full of fire, strength, vibrancy. He could want all of it, have all of it. It wouldn't be enough.

He was an expert at capturing the moment, the emotions, the message. Letting his own feelings hum, he reached for his camera bag.

"What're you doing?"

When she started to sit up, Shade turned back. "Stay there a minute."

Intrigued and wary, she watched him set his camera. "I don't—"

"Just lie back like you were," he interrupted. "Relaxed and rather pleased with yourself."

His intention was obvious enough now. Bryan lifted a brow. An obsession, she thought, amused. The camera was an obsession for both of them. "Shade, I'm a photographer, not a model."

"Humor me." Gently, he pushed her back on the bed.

"I've too much champagne in my system to argue with you." She smiled up at him as he held the camera over his face. "You can play if you like, or take serious pictures if you must. As long as I don't have to do anything."

She did nothing but smile and he began to throb. So often he'd used the camera as a barrier between himself and his subject, other times as a conductor for his emotion, emotion he refused to let loose any other way. Now, it was neither. The emotion was already in him and barriers weren't possible.

He framed her quickly and shot, but was unsatisfied.

"That's not what I want." He was so businesslike that Bryan didn't see it as a defense, only as his manner. But when he came over, pulled her into a sitting position and unzipped her dress, her mouth fell open.

"Shade!"

"It's that lazy sex," he murmured as he slipped the dress down over one shoulder. "Those incredible waves of sensuality that take no effort at all, but just are. It's the way your eyes look." But when his came back to hers, she forgot the joke she'd been about to make. "The way they look when I touch you—like this." Slowly, he ran a hand over her naked shoulder. "The way they look just after I kiss you—like this." He kissed her, lingering over it while her mind emptied of thought and her body filled with sensation.

"Like this," he whispered, more determined than ever to capture that moment, make it tangible so that he could hold it in his hands and see it. "Just like this," he said again, backing off one step, then two. "The way you look just before we make love. The way you look just after."

Helplessly aroused, Bryan stared into the lens of the camera as he lifted it. He caught her there, like a quarry in the cross hairs of a scope, empty of thoughts, jumbled with feeling. At the same time, he caught himself.

For an instant her heart was in her eyes. The shutter opened, closed and captured it. When he printed the photograph, he thought as he carefully set down his camera, would he see what she felt? Would he be certain of his own feelings?

Now she sat on the bed, her dress disarrayed, her hair tumbled, her eyes clouded. Secrets, Shade thought again. They both had them. Was it possible he'd locked a share of each of their secrets on film inside his camera?

When he looked at her now he saw a woman aroused, a woman who aroused. He could see passion and pliancy and acceptance. He could see a woman whom he'd come to know better than anyone else. Yet he saw a woman he'd yet to reach—one he'd avoided reaching.

He went to her in silence. Her skin was damp but warm, as he'd known it would be. Raindrops clung to her hair. He touched one, then it was gone. Her arms lifted.

While the storm raged outside, he took her and himself where there was no need for answers.

Chapter Eleven

If they had more time...

As August began to slip by that was the thought that continued to run through Bryan's mind. With more time, they could have stayed longer at each stop. With more time, they might have passed through more states, more towns, more communities. There was so much to see, so much to record, but time was running out.

In less than a month, the school she'd photographed empty and waiting in the afternoon light would be filled again. Leaves that were full and green would take on those vibrant colors before they fell. She would be back in L.A., back in her studio, back to the routine she'd established. For the first time in years, the word *alone* had a hollow ring.

How had it happened? Shade Colby had become her partner, her lover, her friend. He'd become, though it was frightening to admit, the most important person in her life. Somehow she'd become dependent on him, for his opinion, his company, for the nights they spent involved only with each other.

She could imagine how it would be when they returned to L.A. and went their separate ways. Separate parts of the city, she thought, separate lives, separate outlooks.

The closeness that had so slowly, almost painfully developed between them would dissolve. Wasn't that what they'd both intended from the start? They'd made a bargain with each other, just as they'd made the bargain to work together. If her feelings had changed, she was responsible for them, for dealing with them. As the odometer turned over on the next mile, as the next state was left behind, she wondered how to begin.

Shade had his own thoughts to deal with. When they'd crossed into Maryland, they'd crossed into the east. The Atlantic was close, as close as the end of summer. It was the end that disturbed him. The word no longer seemed to mean finished, but over. He began to realize he was far from ready to draw that last line. There were ways to rationalize it. He tried them all.

They'd missed too much. If they took their time driving back rather than sticking to their plan of going straight across the country, they could detour into so many places they'd eliminated on the way out. It made sense. They could stay in New England a week, two weeks after Labor Day. After long days in the van and the intense work they'd both put in, they deserved some time off. It was reasonable.

They should work their way back rather than rush. If they weren't preoccupied with making time, making miles, how many pictures would come out of it? If one of them were special, it would be worth it. That was professional.

When they returned to L.A., perhaps Bryan could move in with him, share his apartment as they'd shared the van. It was impossible. Wasn't it?

She didn't want to complicate their relationship. Hadn't she said so? He didn't want the responsibility of committing himself to one person. Hadn't he made himself clear? Perhaps he'd come to need her companionship on some level. And it was true he'd learned to appreciate the way she could look at anything and see the fun and the beauty of it. That didn't equal promises, commitments or complications.

With a little time, a little distance, the need was bound to fade. The only thing he was sure of was that he wanted to put off that point for as long as possible.

Bryan spotted a convertible—red, flashy. Its driver had one arm thrown over the white leather seat while her short blond hair flew in the wind. Grabbing her camera, Bryan leaned out the open window. Half kneeling, half crouching on the seat, she adjusted for depth.

She wanted to catch it from the rear, elongating the car into a blur of color. But she didn't want to lose the arrogant angle of the driver's arm, or the negligent way her hair streamed back. Already she knew she would dodge the plain gray highway and the other cars in the darkroom. Just the red convertible, she thought as she set her camera.

"Try to keep just this distance," she called to Shade. She took one shot and, dissatisfied, leaned out farther for the next. Though Shade swore at her, Bryan got her shot before she laughed and flopped back on her seat.

He was guilty of the same thing, he knew. Once the camera was in place you tended to think of it as a shield. Nothing could happen to you—you simply weren't part of what was happening. Though he'd known better, it had happened to him often enough, even after his first stint overseas. Perhaps it was the understanding that made his voice mild, though he was annoyed.

"Don't you have more sense than to climb out the window of a moving car?"

"Couldn't resist. There's nothing like a convertible on an open highway in August. I'm always toying with the idea of getting one myself."

"Why don't you?"

"Buying a new car is hard work." She looked at the green and white road signs as she'd looked at so many others that summer. There were cities, roads and routes she'd never heard of. "I can hardly believe we're in Maryland. We've come so far and yet, I don't know, it doesn't seem like two months."

"Two years?"

She laughed. "Sometimes. Other times it seems like days. Not enough time," she said half to herself. "Never enough."

Shade didn't give himself the chance to think before he took the opening. "We've had to leave out a lot."

"I know."

"We went through Kansas, but not Nebraska, Mississippi, and not the Carolinas. We didn't go to Michigan or Wisconsin."

"Or Florida, Washington State, the Dakotas." She shrugged, trying not to think of what was left behind. Just today, Bryan told herself. Just take today.

"I've been thinking about tying them in on the way back."

"On the way back?" Bryan turned to him as he reached for a cigarette.

"We'd be on our own time." The van's lighter glowed red against the tip. "But I think we could both take a month or so and finish the job."

More time. Bryan felt the quick surge of hope, then ruthlessly toned it down. He wanted to finish the job his way. It was his way, she reminded herself, to do things thoroughly. But did the reason really matter? They'd have more time. Yes, she realized as she stared out the side window. The reason mattered a great deal too much.

"The job's finished in New England," she said lightly. "Summer's over and it's back to business. My work at the studio will be backed up for a month. Still..." She felt herself weakening though he said nothing, did nothing to persuade her. "I wouldn't mind a few detours on the trip back."

Shade kept his hands easy on the wheel, his voice casual. "We'll think about it," he said and let the subject they both wanted to pursue drop.

Weary of the highway, they took to the back roads. Bryan took her pictures of kids squirting each other with garden hoses, of laundry drying in the breeze, of an elderly couple sitting on a porch glider. Shade took his of sweating construction workers spreading tar on roofs, of laborers harvesting peaches and, surprisingly, of two tenyear-old businessmen hawking lemonade in their front yard.

Touched, Bryan accepted the paper cup Shade handed her. "That was sweet."

"You haven't tasted it yet," he commented and climbed into the passenger's seat. "To keep down the overhead, they used a light hand on the sugar."

"I meant you." On impulse she leaned over and kissed him, lightly, comfortably. "You can be a very sweet man."

As always, she moved him, and he couldn't stop it. "I can give you a list of people who'd disagree."

"What do they know?" With a smile, she touched her lips to his again. She drove down the neat, shady street appreciating the trim lawns, flower gardens and dogs barking in the yards. "I like the suburbs," she said idly. "To look at, anyway. I've never lived in one. They're so orderly." With a sigh, she turned right at the corner. "If I had a house here, I'd probably forget to fertilize the lawn and end up with crab grass and dandelions. My neighbors would take up a petition. I'd end up selling my house and moving into a condo."

"So ends Bryan Mitchell's career as a suburbanite."

She made a face at him. "Some people aren't cut out for picket fences."

"True enough."

She waited, but he said nothing that made her feel inadequate—nothing that made her feel as though she should be. She laughed delightedly, then grabbed his hand and squeezed. "You're good for me, Shade. You really are."

He didn't want to let her hand go and released it reluctantly. Good for her. She said it so easily, laughing. Because she did, he knew she had no idea just what it meant to him to hear it. Maybe it was time he told her. "Bryan—"

"What's that?" she said abruptly, and swung toward the curb. Excited, she inched the car forward until she could read the colorful cardboard poster tacked to a telephone pole. "Nightingale's Traveling Carnival." Pulling on the brake, she nearly climbed over Shade to see it more clearly. "Voltara, the Electric Woman." With a half whoop, she nudged closer to Shade. "Terrific, just terrific. Sampson, the Dancing Elephant. Madam Zoltar, Mystic. Shade, look, it's their last night in town. We can't miss it. What's summer without a carny? Thrilling rides, games of skill and chance."

"And Dr. Wren, the Fire Eater."

It was easy to ignore the dry tone. "Fate." She scrambled back to her own seat. "It has to be fate that we turned down this road. Otherwise, we might've missed it."

Shade glanced back at the sign as Bryan pulled away from the curb. "Think of it," he murmured. "We might've gotten all the way to the coast without seeing a dancing elephant."

A half hour later, Shade leaned back in his seat, calmly smoking, his feet on the dash. Frazzled, Bryan swung the van around the next turn.

"I'm not lost."

Shade blew out a lazy stream of smoke. "I didn't say a word."

"I know what you're thinking."

"That's Madam Zoltar's line."

"And you can stop looking so smug."

"Was I?"

"You always look smug when I get lost."

"You said you weren't."

Bryan gritted her teeth and sent him a killing look. "Why don't you just pick up that map and tell me where we are?"

"I started to pick it up ten minutes ago and you snarled at me."

Bryan let out a long breath. "It was the *way* you picked it up. You were smirking, and I could hear you thinking—"

"You're stepping into Madam Zoltar's territory again."

"Damn it, Shade." But she had to choke back a laugh as she drove down the long, unlit country road. "I don't mind making a fool of myself, but I hate it when someone lifts an eyebrow over it."

"Did I?"

"You know you did. Now, if you'd just—"

Then she caught the first glimmer of red, blue, green lights flickering. A Ferris wheel, she thought. It had to be. The sound of tinny music came faintly through the summer dusk. A calliope. This time it was Bryan who looked smug. "I knew I'd find it."

"I never had a doubt."

She might've had something withering to say to that, but the lights glowing in the early evening dusk, and the foolish piping music held her attention. "It's been years," she murmured. "Just years since I've seen anything like this. I've got to watch the fire eater."

"And your wallet."

She shook her head as she turned off the road onto the bumpy field where cars were parked. "Cynic."

"Realist." He waited until she maneuvered the van next to a late-model pickup. "Lock the van." Shade gathered his bag and waited outside the van until Bryan had hers. "Where first?"

She thought of pink cotton candy but restrained herself. "Why don't we just wander around a bit? We might want some shots now, but at night they'd have more punch."

Without the dark, without the bright glow of colored lights, the carnival looked too much like what it was—a little weary, more than a little tawdry. Its illusions were too easily unmasked now, and that wasn't why Bryan had come. Carnivals, like Santa Claus, had a right to their mystique. In another hour, when the sun had completely set behind those rolling, blue-tinted hills to the west, the carnival would come into its own. Peeling paint wouldn't be noticed.

"Look, there's Voltara." Bryan grabbed Shade's arm and swung him around to see a life-size poster that gave her lavish curves and scant cover as she was being strapped into what looked like a homemade electric chair.

Shade looked at the painted spangles over generous cleavage. "Might be worth watching after all."

With a quick snort, Bryan pulled him toward the Ferris wheel. "Let's take a ride. From the top we'll be able to see the whole layout."

Shade pulled a bill out of his wallet. "That's the only reason you want to ride."

"Don't be ridiculous." They walked over, waiting while the attendant let a couple off. "It's a good way of covering ground and sitting down at the same time," she began as she took the vacated seat. "It's sure to be an excellent angle for some aerial pictures, and..." She slipped a hand into his as they started the slow swing up. "It's the very best place to neck at a carnival."

When he laughed, she wrapped her arms around him and silenced his lips with hers. They reached the top where the evening breeze flowed clean and hung there one moment—two—aware only of each other. On the descent, the speed picked up and the drop had her stomach shivering, her mind swimming. It was no different from the sensation of being held by him, loved by him. They held tight and close through two revolutions.

Gathering her against his shoulder, Shade watched the carnival rush up toward them. It'd been years since he'd held someone soft and feminine on a Ferris wheel. High school? he wondered. He could hardly remember. Now he realized he'd let his youth slip by him because so many other things had seemed important at the time. He'd let it go freely and though he wouldn't, couldn't, ask for the whole of it back, perhaps Bryan was showing him how to recapture pieces of it.

"I love the way this feels," she murmured. She could watch the sun go down in a last splashy explosion of arrogance, hear the music, the voices ebb and fade as the wheel spun around. She could look down and be just removed enough from the scene to enjoy it, just separate enough to understand it. "A ride on a Ferris wheel should be required once a year, like a routine physical."

With her head against Shade's shoulder she examined the scene below, the midway, the concessions, the booths set up for games of skill. She wanted to see it all, close up. She could smell popcorn, grilling meat, sweat, the heavy-handed after-shave of the attendant as their car swung by him. It gave her the overall view. This was life, a side-long glance at it. This was the little corner of life where children could see wonders and adults could pretend for just a little while.

Taking her camera, she angled down through the cars and wires to focus in on the attendant. He looked a bit bored as he lifted the safety bar for one couple and lowered it for the next. A job for him, Bryan thought, a small thrill for the rest. She sat back, content to ride.

When it was dark, they went to work. There were people gathered around the Wheel of Fortune, plopping down a dollar for a chance at more. Teenagers showed off for their girls or their peers by hurling softballs at stacked bottles. Toddlers hung over the rope and tossed ping-pong balls at fishbowls, hoping to win a goldfish whose life expectancy was short at best. Young girls squealed on the fast-spinning Octopus while young boys goggled at the posters along the midway.

Bryan took one telling shot of a woman carrying a baby on one hip while a three-year-old dragged her mercilessly along. Shade took another of a trio of boys in muscle shirts standing apart and doing their best to look tough and aloof.

They ate slices of pizza with rubber crusts as they watched with the rest of the crowd as Dr. Wren, Fire

Eater, came out of his tent to give a quick, teasing demonstration of his art. Like the ten-year-old boy who watched beside her, Bryan was sold.

With an agreement to meet back at the entrance to the midway in thirty minutes, they separated. Caught up, Bryan wandered. She wasn't able to resist Voltara and slipped into part of the show to see the somewhat weary, glossy-faced woman strapped into a chair that promised to zap her with two thousand volts.

She pulled it off well enough, Bryan thought, closing her eyes and giving a regal nod before the lever was pulled. The special effects weren't top-notch, but they worked. Blue light shimmered up the chair and around Voltara's head. It turned her skin to the color of summer lightning. At fifty cents a shot, Bryan decided as she stepped back out, the audience got their money's worth.

Intrigued, she wandered around in back of the midway to where the carnival workers parked their trailers. No colorful lights here, she mused as she glanced over the small caravan. No pretty illusions. Tonight, they'd pack up the equipment, take down the posters and drive on.

The moonlight hit the metal of a trailer and showed the scratches and dents. The shades were drawn at the little windows, but there was faded lettering on the side. Nightingale's.

Bryan found it touching and crouched to shoot.

"Lost, little lady?"

Surprised, Bryan sprang up and nearly collided with a short, husky man in T-shirt and work pants. If he worked for the carnival, Bryan thought quickly, he'd been taking a long break. If he'd come to watch, the lights and sideshows hadn't held his interest. The smell of beer, warm and stale, clung to him.

"No." She gave him a careful smile and kept a careful distance. Fear hadn't entered into it. The move had been automatic and mild. There were lights and people only a few yards away. And she thought he might give her another angle for his photographs. "Do you work here?"

"Woman shouldn't wander around in the dark alone. 'Less she's looking for something."

No, fear hadn't been her first reaction, nor did it come now. Annoyance did. It was that that showed in her eyes before she turned away. "Excuse me."

Then he had her arm and it occurred to her that the lights were a great deal farther away than she'd have liked. Brazen it out, she told herself. "Look, I've people waiting for me."

"You're a tall one, ain't you?" His fingers were very firm, if his stance wasn't. He weaved slightly as he looked Bryan over. "Don't mind looking eye to eye with a woman. Let's have a drink."

"Some other time." Bryan put her hand on his arm to push it away and found it solid as a concrete block. That's when the fear began. "I came back here to take some pictures," she said as calmly as she could. "My partner's waiting for me." She pushed at his arm again. "You're hurting me."

"Got some more beer in my truck," he mumbled as he began to drag her farther away from the lights.

"No." Her voice rose on the first wave of panic. "I don't want any beer."

He stopped a moment, swaying. As Bryan took a good look in his eyes she realized he was as drunk as a man could get and still stand. Fear bubbled hot in her throat. "Maybe you want something else." He skimmed down her thin summer top and brief shorts. "Woman usually wants something when she wanders around half naked."

Her fear ebbed as cold fury rushed in. Bryan glared. He grinned.

"You ignorant ass," she hissed just before she brought her knee up, hard. His breath came out in a whoosh as he dropped his hand. Bryan didn't wait to see him crouch over. She ran.

She was still running when she rammed straight into Shade.

"You're ten minutes late," he began, "but I've never seen you move that fast."

"I was just—I had to..." She trailed off, breathless, and leaned against him. Solid, dependable, safe. She could have stayed just like that until the sun rose again.

"What is it?" He could feel the tension before he drew her away and saw it on her face. "What happened?"

"Nothing really." Disgusted with herself, Bryan dragged her hair back from her face. "I just ran into some jerk who wanted to buy me a drink whether I was thirsty or not."

His fingers tightened on her arms and she winced as they covered the same area that was already tender. "Where?"

"It was nothing," she said again, furious with herself that she hadn't taken the time to regain her composure before she ran into him. "I went around back to get a look at the trailers."

"Alone?" He shook her once, quickly. "What kind of idiot are you? Don't you know carnivals aren't just cotton candy and colored lights? Did he hurt you?"

It wasn't concern she heard in his voice, but anger. Her spine straightened. "No, but you are."

Ignoring her, Shade began to drag her through the crowds toward the parking section. "If you'd stop looking at everything through rose-colored glasses, you'd see a lot more clearly. Do you have any idea what might've happened?''

''I can take care of myself. I did take care of myself.''
When they reached the van she swung away from him.
''I'll look at life any way I like. I don't need you to lecture me, Shade.''

''You need something.'' Grabbing the keys from her, he unlocked the van. ''It's brainless to go wandering around alone in the dark in a place like this. Looking for trouble,'' he muttered as he climbed into the driver's seat.

''You sound remarkably like the idiot I left sprawled on the grass with his hands between his legs.''

He shot her a look. Later, when he was calm, he might admire the way she'd dealt with an obnoxious drunk, but now he couldn't see beyond her carelessness. Independence aside, a woman was vulnerable. ''I should've known better than to let you go off alone.''

''Now just a minute.'' She whirled around in her seat. ''You don't *let* me do anything, Colby. If you've got it in your head that you're my keeper or anything of the sort then you'd better get it right out again. I answer to myself. Only myself.''

''For the next few weeks, you answer to me as well.''

She tried to control the temper that pushed at her, but it wasn't possible. ''I may work with you,'' she said, pacing her words. ''I may sleep with you. But I don't answer to you. Not now. Not ever.''

Shade punched in the van's lighter. ''We'll see about that.''

''Just remember the contract.'' Shaking with fury, she turned away again. ''We're partners on this job, fifty-fifty.''

He gave his opinion of what to do with the contract. Bryan folded her arms, shut her eyes and willed herself to sleep.

He drove for hours. She might sleep, but there was too much churning inside him to allow him the same release. So he drove, east toward the Atlantic.

She'd been right when she'd said she didn't answer to him. That was one of the first rules they'd laid down. He was damned sick of rules. She was her own woman. His strings weren't on her any more than hers were on him. They were two intelligent, independent people who wanted it that way.

But he'd wanted to protect her. When everything else was stripped away, he'd wanted to protect her. Was she so dense that she couldn't see he'd been furious not with her but with himself for not being there when she'd needed him?

She'd tossed that back in his face, Shade thought grimly as he ran a hand over his gritty eyes. She'd put him very clearly, very concisely in his place. And his place, he reminded himself, no matter how intimate they'd become, was still at arm's length. It was best for both of them.

With his window open, he could just smell the tang of the ocean. They'd crossed the country. They'd crossed more lines than he'd bargained for. But they were a long way from crossing the final one.

How did he feel about her? He'd asked himself that question time after time, but he'd always managed to block out the answer. Did he really want to hear it? But it was three o'clock in the morning, that hour he knew well. Defenses crumbled easily at three o'clock in the morning. Truth had a way of easing its way in.

He was in love with her. It was too late to take a step back and say no thanks. He was in love with her in a way that was completely foreign to him. Unselfishly. Unlimitedly.

Looking back, he could almost pinpoint the moment when it had happened to him, though he'd called it something else. When he'd stood on the rock island in the Arizona lake he'd desired her, desired her more intensely than he'd desired anything or anyone. When he'd woken from the nightmare and had found her warm and solid beside him, he'd needed her, again more than anything or anyone.

But when he'd looked across the dusty road on the Oklahoma border and seen her standing in front of a sad little house with a plot of pansies, he'd fallen in love.

They were a long way from Oklahoma now, a long way from that moment. Love had grown, overwhelming him. He hadn't known how to deal with it then. He hadn't a clue what to do about it now.

He drove toward the ocean where the air was moist. When he pulled the van between two low-rising dunes he could just see the water, a shadow with sound in the distance. Watching it, listening to it, he slept.

Bryan woke when she heard the gulls. Stiff, disoriented, she opened her eyes. She saw the ocean, blue and quiet in the early light that wasn't quite dawn. At the horizon the sky was pink and serene. Misty. Waking slowly, she watched gulls swoop over the shoreline and soar to sea again.

Shade slept in the seat beside her, turned slightly in his seat, his head resting against the door. He'd driven for hours, she realized. But what had driven him?

She thought of their argument with a kind of weary tolerance. Quietly, she slipped from the van. She wanted the scent of the sea.

Had it only been two months since they'd stood on the shore of the Pacific? Was this really so different? she wondered as she stepped out of her shoes and felt the sand cool and rough under her feet. He'd driven through the night to get here, she mused. To get here, one step closer to the end. They had only to drive up the coast now, winding their way through New England. A quick stop in New York for pictures and darkroom work, then on to Cape Cod where summer would end for both of them.

It might be best, she thought, if they broke there completely. Driving back together, touching off on some of the places they'd discovered as a team might be too much to handle. Perhaps when the time came, she'd make some excuse and fly back to L.A. It might be best, she reflected, to start back to those separate lives when summer ended.

They'd come full circle. Through the tension and annoyance of the beginning, into the cautious friendship, the frenzied passion and right back to the tension again.

Bending, Bryan picked up a shell small enough to fit into the palm of her hand, but whole.

Tension broke things, didn't it? Cracked the whole until pressure crumbled it into pieces. Then whatever you'd had was lost. She didn't want that for Shade. With a sigh, she looked out over the ocean where the water was green, then blue. The mist was rising.

No, she didn't want that for him. When they turned from each other, they should do so as they'd turned to each other. As whole, separate people, standing independently.

She kept the shell in her hand as she walked back toward the van. The weariness was gone. When she saw him standing beside the van watching her, with his hair ruffled by the wind, his face shadowed, eyes heavy, her heart turned over.

The break would come soon enough, she told herself. For now, there should be no pressure.

Smiling, she went to him. She took his hand and pressed the shell into it. "You can hear the ocean if you listen for it."

He said nothing, but put his arm around her and held her. Together they watched the sun rise over the east.

Chapter Twelve

On a street corner in Chelsea, five enterprising kids loosened the bolts on a fire hydrant and sent water swooshing. Bryan liked the way they dived through the stream, soaking their sneakers, plastering their hair. It wasn't necessary to think long about her feelings toward the scene. As she lifted her camera and focused, her one predominant emotion was envy, pure and simple.

Not only were they cool and delightfully wet while she was limp from the heat, but they hadn't a care in the world. They didn't have to worry if their lives were heading in the right direction, or any direction at all. It was their privilege in these last breathless weeks of summer to enjoy—their youth, their freedom and a cool splash in city water.

If she were envious, there were others who felt the same way. As it happened, Bryan's best shot came from incorporating one passerby in the scene. The middle-aged delivery man in the sweaty blue shirt and dusty work shoes looked over his shoulder as one of the children lifted his arms up to catch a stream. On one face was pleasure, pure and giddy. On the other was amusement laced with regret for something that couldn't be recaptured.

Bryan walked on, down streets packed with bad-tempered traffic, over sidewalks that tossed up heat like insults. New York didn't always weather summer with a smile and a wave.

Shade was in the darkroom they'd rented while she'd opted to take the field first. She was putting it off, she admitted, as she skirted around a sidewalk salesman and his array of plastic, bright-lensed sunglasses. Putting off coping with the last darkroom session she'd have before they returned to California. After this brief stop in New York, they'd head north for the final weekend of summer in Cape Cod.

And she and Shade had gone back to being almost unbearably careful with each other. Since that morning when they'd woken at the beach, Bryan had taken a step back. Deliberately, she admitted. She'd discovered all too forcibly that he could hurt her. Perhaps it was true that she'd left herself wide open. Bryan wouldn't deny that somewhere along the way she'd lost her determination to maintain a certain distance. But it wasn't too late to pull back just enough to keep from getting battered. She had to accept that the season was nearly over, and when it was, her relationship with Shade ended with it.

With this in mind, she took a slow, meandering route back toward midtown and the rented darkroom.

Shade already had ten rows of proofs. Sliding a strip under the enlarger, he methodically began to select and eliminate. As always, he was more ruthless, more critical with his own work than he'd have been with anyone else's. He knew Bryan would be back shortly so that any printing he did would have to wait until the following day. Still, he wanted to see one now for himself.

He remembered the little motel room they'd taken that rainy night just outside of Louisville. He remembered the way he'd felt then—involved, a little reckless. That night had been preying on his mind, more and more often as he and Bryan seemed to put up fences again. There'd been no boundaries between them that night.

Finding the print he was looking for, he brought the magnifier closer. She was sitting on the bed, her dress falling off her shoulders, raindrops clinging to her hair. Soft, passionate, hesitant. All those things were there in the way she held herself, in the way she looked at the camera. But her eyes . . .

Frustrated, he narrowed his own. What was in her eyes? He wanted to enlarge the proof now, to blow it up so that he could see and study and understand.

She was holding back now. Every day he could feel it, sense it. Just a little bit more distance every day. But what had been in her eyes on that rainy night? He had to know. Until he did, he couldn't take a step, either toward her or away.

When the knock came on the door, he cursed it. He wanted another hour. With another hour he could have the print, and perhaps his answer. He found it a simple matter to ignore the knock.

"Shade, come on. Time for the next shift."

"Come back in an hour."

"An hour!" On the other side of the door, Bryan pounded again. "Look, I'm melting out there. Besides, I've already given you twenty minutes more than your share."

The moment he yanked open the door, Bryan felt the waves of impatience. Because she wasn't in the mood to wrestle with it, she merely lifted a brow and skirted around him. If he wanted to be in a foul mood, fine. As long as he took it outside with him. Casually she set down her camera and a paper cup filled with soft drink and ice.

"So how'd it go?"

"I'm not finished."

With a shrug, she began to set out the capsules of undeveloped film she'd stored in her bag. "You've tomorrow for that."

He didn't want to wait until tomorrow, not, he discovered, for another minute. "If you'd give me the rest of the time I want I wouldn't need tomorrow."

Bryan began to run water in a shallow plastic tub. "Sorry, Shade. I've run out of steam outside. If I don't get started in here, the best I'll do is go back to the hotel and sleep the rest of the afternoon. Then I'll be behind. What's so important?"

He stuffed his hands in his pockets. "Nothing. I just want to finish."

"And I've got to start," she murmured absently as she checked the temperature of the water.

He watched her a moment, the competent way she set up, arranging bottles of chemicals to her preference. Little tendrils of her hair curled damply around her face from the humidity. Even as she set up to work, she slipped out of her shoes. He felt a wave of love, of need, of confusion, and reached out to touch her shoulder. "Bryan—"

"Hmm?"

He started to move closer, then stopped himself. "What time will you be finished?"

There were touches of amusement and annoyance in her voice. "Shade, will you stop trying to push me out?"

"I want to come back for you."

She stopped long enough to look over her shoulder. "Why?"

"Because I don't want you walking around outside after it's dark."

"For heaven's sake." Exasperated, she turned completely around. "Do you have any idea how many times I've been to New York alone? Do I look stupid?"

"No."

Something in the way he said it had her narrowing her eyes. "Look—"

"I want to come back for you," he repeated and this time touched her cheek. "Humor me."

She let out a long breath, tried to be annoyed and ended by lifting her hand to his. "Eight, eight-thirty."

"Okay. We can grab something to eat on the way back."

"There's something we can agree on." She smiled and lowered her hand before she could give in to the urge to move closer. "Now go take some pictures, will you? I've got to get to work."

He lifted his camera bag and started out. "Any longer than eight-thirty and you buy dinner."

Bryan locked the door behind him with a decisive click.

She didn't lose track of time while she worked. Time was too essential. In the dark she worked briskly. In the amber light her movements flowed with the same rhythm. As one set of negatives was developed and hung to dry, she went on to the next, then the next. When at length she could switch on the overhead light, Bryan arched her back, stretched her shoulders and relaxed.

An idle glance around showed her that she'd forgotten the carry-out drink she'd picked up on the way. Unconcerned, she took a long gulp of lukewarm, watered-down soda.

The work satisfied her—the precision it required. Now her thoughts were skipping ahead to the prints. Only then would the creativity be fully satisfied. She had time, she noticed as she took a quick glance at her watch, to fuss with the negatives a bit before he came back. But then she'd end up putting herself in the same position she'd put him in—leaving something half done. Instead, mildly curious, she walked over to study his proofs.

Impressive, she decided, but then she'd expected no less. She might just be inclined to beg for a blowup of the old man in the baseball cap. Not Shade's usual style, she mused as she bent over the strip. It was so rare that he focused in on one person and let the emotions flow. The man who'd taken it had once told her he had no compassion. Bryan shook her head as she skimmed over other proofs. Did Shade believe that, or did he simply want the rest of the world to?

Then she saw herself and stopped with a kind of dazed wonder. Of course she remembered Shade setting up that picture, amusing, then arousing her while he changed angles and f-stops. The way he'd touched her... It wasn't something she'd forget, so it shouldn't surprise her to see the proof. Yet it did more than surprise her.

Not quite steady, Bryan picked up a magnifying glass and held it over one tiny square. She looked...pliant. She heard her own nervous swallow as she looked deeper. She looked...soft. It could be her imagination or, more likely, the skill of the photographer. She looked . . . in love.

Slowly, Bryan set down the glass and straightened. The skill of the photographer, she repeated, fighting to believe it. A trick of the angle, of the light and shadows. What a photographer captured on film wasn't always the truth. It was often illusion, often that vague blur between truth and illusion.

A woman knew when she loved. That's what Bryan told herself. A woman knew when she'd given her heart. It wasn't something that could happen and not be felt.

She closed her eyes a moment and listened to the quiet. Was there anything she hadn't felt when it came to Shade? How much longer was she going to pretend that passion, needs, longings stood on their own? Love had bound them together. Love had cemented them into something solid and strong and undeniable.

She turned to where her negatives hung. There was one she'd managed to ignore. There was one tiny slice of film she'd taken on impulse and then buried because she'd come to be afraid of the answer she'd find. Now, when she had the answer already, Bryan stared at it.

It was reversed, so that his hair was light, his face dark. The little sliver of river in the corner was white, like the oars in his hands. But she saw him clearly.

His eyes were too intense, though his body seemed relaxed. Would he ever allow his mind true rest? His face was hard, lean, with the only tangible sensitivity around his mouth. He was a man, Bryan knew, who'd have little patience with mistakes—his own or others'. He was a man with a rigid sense of what was important. And he was a man who was capable of harnessing his own emotions and denying them to another. What he gave, when he gave, would be on his terms.

She knew, and understood, and loved regardless.

She'd loved before, and love had made more sense then. At least it had seemed to. Still, in the end love hadn't been enough. What did she know about making love work? Could she possibly believe that when she'd failed once, she could succeed with a man like Shade?

She loved now and told herself she was wise enough, strong enough, to let him go.

Rule number one, Bryan reminded herself as she put the darkroom in order. No complications. It was a litany she had running through her head until Shade knocked on the door. When she opened it for him, she nearly believed it.

They'd reached the last stop, the last day. Summer was not, as some would wish it, endless. Perhaps the weather would stay balmy for weeks longer. Flowers might still bloom defiantly, but just as Bryan had considered the last day of school summer's conception, so did she consider the Labor Day weekend its demise.

Clambakes, beach parties, bonfires. Hot beaches and cool water. That was Cape Cod. There were volleyball games in the sand and blasting portable radios. Teenagers perfected the tans they'd show off during those first few weeks of school. Families took to the water in a last, frantic rush before autumn signaled the end. Backyard barbecues smoked. Baseball hung on gamely before football could push its way through. As if it knew its time was limited, summer poured on the heat.

Bryan didn't mind. She wanted this last weekend to be everything summer could be—hot, hazy, torrid. She wanted her last weekend with Shade to reflect it. Love could be disguised with passion. She could let herself flow with it. Long steamy days led to long, steamy nights and Bryan held on to them.

If her lovemaking was a little frantic, her desires a little desperate, she could blame it on the heat. While Bryan became more aggressive, Shade became more gentle.

He'd noticed the change. Though he'd said nothing, Shade had noticed it the night he'd come back to meet her at the darkroom. Perhaps because she rarely had nerves, Bryan thought she hid them well. Shade could almost see them jump every time he looked at her.

Bryan had made a decision in the darkroom—a decision she felt would be best for both herself and for Shade.

Shade had made a decision in the darkroom as well, the day after, when he'd watched the print of Bryan slowly come to life.

On the ride west to east they'd become lovers. Now he had to find a way on the ride east to court her, as a man does the woman he wants to spend his life with.

Gentleness came first, though he wasn't an expert at it. Pressure, if it came to that, could be applied later. He was more experienced there.

"What a day." After long hours walking, watching and shooting, Bryan dropped down on the back of the van where the doors were open wide to let in the breeze. "I can't believe how many half-naked people I've seen." Grinning at Shade, she arched her back. She wore nothing but her sleek red bathing suit and a loose white cover-up that drooped over one shoulder.

"You seem to fit right in."

Lazily, she lifted one leg and examined it. "Well, it's nice to know that this assignment hasn't ruined my tan." Yawning, she stretched. "We've got a couple more hours of sun. Why don't you put on something indecent and walk down to the beach with me?" She rose, lifting her arms so they could wind easily around his neck. "We could cool off in the water." She touched her lips to his, teasing, taunting. "Then we could come back and heat up again."

"I like the second part." He turned the kiss into something staggering with an increase of pressure and change of angle. Beneath his hands, he felt her sigh. "Why don't you go ahead down, do the cooling off? I've got some things to do."

With her head resting against his shoulder Bryan struggled not to ask again. She wanted him to go with her, be with her every second they had left. Tomorrow she'd have to tell him that she'd made arrangements to fly back to the coast. This was their last night, but only she knew it.

"All right." She managed to smile as she drew away. "I can't resist the beach when we're camped so close. I'll be back in a couple hours."

"Have fun." He gave her a quick, absent kiss and didn't watch as she walked away. If he had, he might've seen her hesitate and start back once, only to turn around again and walk on.

The air had cooled by the time Bryan started back to the van. It chilled her skin, a sure sign that summer was on its last legs. Bonfires were set and ready to light down on the beach. In the distance, Bryan heard a few hesitant, amateur guitar chords. It wouldn't be a quiet night, she decided as she passed two other campsites on the way to the van.

She paused a moment to look toward the water, tossing her hair back. It was loose from its braid and slightly damp from her dip in the Atlantic. Idly she considered grabbing her shampoo out of the van and taking a quick trip to the showers. She could do that before she threw together a cold sandwich. In an hour or two, when the bonfires were going steadily, and the music was at its peak, she and Shade would go back down and work.

For the last time, she thought as she reached for the door of the van.

At first, she stood blinking, confused by the low, flickering light. Candles, she saw, baffled. Candles and white linen. There on the little collapsible table they sometimes set between the bunks was a fresh, snowy cloth and two red tapers in glass holders. There were red linen napkins folded at angles. A rosebud stood in a narrow, clear glass vase. On the little radio in the back was low, soft music.

At the narrow makeshift counter was Shade, legs spread as he added a sprinkling of alfalfa to a salad.

"Have a nice swim?" he said casually, as if she'd climbed into the van every evening to just such a scene.

"Yeah, I... Shade, where did you get all this?"

"Took a quick trip into town. Hope you like your shrimp spicy. I made it to my taste."

She could smell it. Over the scent of candle wax, under the fragrance of the single rose, was the rich, ripe aroma of spiced shrimp. With a laugh, Bryan moved to the table and ran a finger down one of the tapers. "How did you manage all this?"

"I've been called adept occasionally." She looked up from the candle to him. Her face was lovely, clean lined. In the soft light her eyes were dark, mysterious. But above all he saw her lips curve hesitantly as she reached out for him.

"You did this for me."

He touched her, lightly, just a hand to her hair. Both of them felt something shimmer. "I intend to eat, too."

"I don't know what to say." She felt her eyes fill and didn't bother to blink the tears back. "I really don't."

He lifted her hand and, with a simplicity he'd never shown, kissed her fingers, one by one. "Try thanks."

She swallowed and whispered. "Thanks."

"Hungry?"

"Always. But..." In a gesture that always moved him, she lifted her hands to his face. "Some things are more important."

Bryan brought her lips to his. It was a taste he could drown in—a taste he could now admit he wanted to drown in. Moving slowly, gently, he brought her into his arms.

Their bodies fit. Bryan knew it was so and ached from the knowledge. Even their breathing seemed to merge until she was certain their hearts beat at precisely the same rhythm. He ran his hands under her shirt, along her back where the skin was still damp from the sea.

Touch me. She drew him closer as if her body could shout the words to him.

Savor me. Her mouth was suddenly avid, hot and open as if with lips alone she could draw what she needed from him.

Love me. Her hands moved over him as if she could touch the emotion she wanted. Touch it, hold it, keep it— if only for one night.

He could smell the sea on her, and the summer and the evening. He could feel the passion as her body pressed against his. Needs, demands, desires—they could be tasted as his mouth drew from hers. But tonight he found he needed to hear the words. Too soon, his mind warned as he began to lose himself. It was too soon to ask, too soon to tell. She'd need time, he thought, time and more finesse than he was accustomed to employing.

But even when he drew her away, he wasn't able to let go. Looking down at her, he saw his own beginning. Whatever he'd seen and done in the past, whatever memories he had were unimportant. There was only one vital thing in his life and he held it in his arms.

"I want to make love with you."

Her breath was already unsteady, her body trembling. "Yes."

His hands tightened on her as he tried to be logical. "Room's at a premium."

This time she smiled and drew him closer. "We have the floor." She pulled him down with her.

Later, when her mind was clearer and her blood cooler, Bryan would remember only the tumult of feeling, only the flood of sensation. She wouldn't be able to separate the dizzying feel of his mouth on her skin from the heady taste of his under hers.

She'd know that his passion had never been more intense, more relentless, but she wouldn't be able to say how she'd known. Had it been the frantic way he'd said her name? Had it been the desperate way he'd pulled the snug suit down her body, exploiting, ravishing as he went?

She understood her own feelings had reached an apex she could never express with words. Words were inadequate. She could only show him. Love, regrets, desires, wishes had all culminated to whirl inside her until she'd clung to him. And when they'd given each other all they could, she clung still, holding the moment to her as she might a photograph faded after years of looking.

As she lay against him, her head on his chest, she smiled. They had given each other all they could. What more could anyone ask? With her eyes still closed, she pressed her lips against his chest. Nothing would spoil the night. Tonight they'd have candlelight and laughter. She'd never forget it.

"I hope you bought plenty of shrimp," she murmured. "I'm starving."

"I bought enough to feed an average person and a greedy one."

Grinning, she sat up. "Good." With a rare show of energy, she struggled back into the bulky cover-up and sprang up. Bending over the pot of shrimp, she breathed deep. "Wonderful. I didn't know you were so talented."

"I decided it was time I let you in on some of my more admirable qualities."

With a half smile, she looked back to see him slipping on his shorts. "Oh?"

"Yeah. After all, we've got to travel a long way together yet." He sent her a quiet, enigmatic look. "A long way."

"I don't—" She stopped herself and turned to toy with the salad. "This looks good," she began, too brightly.

"Bryan." He stopped her before she could reach in the cupboard above for bowls. "What is it?"

"Nothing." Did he always have to see? she demanded. Couldn't she hide anything from him?

He stepped over, took her arms and held her face to face. "What?"

"Let's talk about it tomorrow, all right?" The brightness was still there, straining. "I'm really hungry. The shrimp's cool by now so—"

"Now." With a quick shake, he reminded both of them that his patience only stretched so far.

"I've decided to fly back," she blurted out. "I can get a flight out tomorrow afternoon."

He went very still but she was too busy working out her explanation to notice just how dangerously still. "Why?"

"I've had to reschedule like crazy to fit in this assignment. The extra time I'd get would ease things." It sounded weak. It was weak.

"Why?"

She opened her mouth, prepared to give him a variation on the same theme. One look from him stopped her. "I just want to get back," she managed. "I know you'd like company on the drive, but the assignment's finished. Odds are you'll make better time without me."

He fought back the anger. Anger wasn't the way. If he'd given in to it, he'd have shouted, raged, threatened. That wasn't the way. "No," he said simply and left it at that.

"No?"

"You're not flying back tomorrow." His voice was calm, but his eyes said a great deal more. "We go together, Bryan."

She braced herself. An argument, she decided, would be easy. "Now look—"

"Sit down."

Haughtiness came to her rarely, but when it did, it was exceptional. "I beg your pardon?"

For an answer, Shade gave her a quick shove onto the bench. Without speaking he pulled open a drawer and took out the manila envelope that held his most recently developed prints. Tossing them onto the table, he pulled out the one of Bryan.

"What do you see?" he demanded.

"Myself." She cleared her throat. "I see myself, of course."

"Not good enough."

"That's what I see," she tossed back, but she didn't look down at the print again. "That's all there is."

Perhaps fear played a part in his actions. He didn't want to admit it. But it was fear, fear that he'd imagined something that wasn't there. "You see yourself, yes. A beautiful woman, a desirable woman. A woman," he continued slowly, "looking at the man she loves."

He'd stripped her. Bryan felt it as though he'd actually peeled off layer after layer of pretense, defense, disguise. She'd seen the same thing in the image he'd frozen on film. She'd seen it, but what gave him the right to strip her?

"You take too much," she said in a quiet voice. Rising, she turned away from him. "Too damned much."

Relief poured through him. He had to close his eyes on it for a moment. Not imagination, not illusion, but truth. Love was there, and with it, his beginning. "You've already given it."

"No." Bryan turned back, holding on to what she had left. "I haven't given it. What I feel is my responsibility. I haven't asked you for anything, and I won't." She took a deep breath. "We agreed, Shade. No complications."

"Then it looks like we both reneged, doesn't it?" He grabbed her hand before she could move out of reach. "Look at me." His face was close, candlelight flickering over it. Somehow the soft light illuminated what he'd seen, what he'd lived through, what he'd overcome. "Don't you see anything when you look at me? Can you see more in a stranger on the beach, a woman in a crowd, a kid on a street corner than you do when you look at me?"

"Don't—" she began, only to be cut off.

"What do you see?"

"I see a man," she said, speaking quickly, passionately. "A man who's had to see more than he should. I see a man who's learned to keep his feelings carefully controlled because he isn't quite sure what would happen if he let loose. I see a cynic who hasn't been able to completely stamp out his own sensitivity, his own empathy."

"True enough," he returned evenly, though it was both more and less than he'd wanted to hear. "What else?"

"Nothing," she told him, close to panic. "Nothing."

It wasn't enough. The frustration came through; she could feel it in his hands. "Where's your perception now? Where's the insight that takes you under the glitter of some temperamental leading man to the core? I want you to see into me, Bryan.''

''I can't.'' The words came out on a shudder. ''I'm afraid to.''

Afraid? He'd never considered it. She took emotions in stride, sought them, dug for them. He loosened his grip on her and said the words that were the most difficult for him to speak. ''I love you.''

She felt the words slam into her, knocking her breathless. If he said them, he meant them, of that she could be sure. Had she been so caught up in her own feelings that she hadn't seen his? It was tempting, it would be easy, to simply go into his arms and take the risk. But she remembered that they'd both risked before, and failed.

''Shade...'' She tried to think calmly but his words of love still rang in her head. ''I don't—you can't—''

''I want to hear you say it.'' He held her close again. There was no place to go. ''I want you to look at me, knowing everything you've said about me is true, and tell me.''

''It couldn't work,'' she began quickly because her knees were shaking. ''It couldn't, don't you see? I'd want it all because I'm just idiot enough to think maybe this time—with you... Marriage, children, that's not what you want, and I understand. I didn't think I wanted them either until everything got so out of control.''

He was calmer now as she became more frazzled. ''You haven't told me yet.''

''All right.'' She nearly shouted it. ''All right then, I love you, but I—''

He closed his mouth over hers so there could be no excuses. For now, he could simply drink in the words and all they meant to him. Salvation. He could believe in it.

"You've a hell of a nerve," he said against her mouth, "telling me what I want."

"Shade, please." Giving in to the weakness, she dropped her head on his shoulder. "I didn't want to complicate things. I don't want to now. If I fly back, it'll give us both time to put things back in perspective. My work, your work—"

"Are important," he finished. "But not as important as this." He waited until her eyes slowly lifted to his. Now his voice was calm again. His grip eased, still holding her but without the desperation. "Nothing is, Bryan. You didn't want it, maybe I thought I didn't, but I know better now. Everything started with you. Everything important. You make me clean." He ran a hand through her hair. "God, you make me hope again, believe again. Do you think I'm going to let you take all that away from me?"

The doubts began to fade, quietly, slowly. Second chances? Hadn't she always believed in them? Long shots, she remembered. You only had to want to win badly enough.

"No," she murmured. "But I need a promise. I need the promise, Shade, and then I think we could do anything."

So did he. "I promise to love you, to respect you. To care for you whether you like it or not. And I promise that what I am is yours." Reaching up, he flipped open the cupboard door. Speechless, Bryan watched him draw out a tiny cardboard pot of pansies. Their scent was light and sweet and lasting.

"Plant them with me, Bryan."

Her hands closed over his. Hadn't she always believed life was as simple as you made it? "As soon as we're home."

Epilogue

Cooperate, will you?"

"No." Amused, but not altogether pleased, Shade watched Bryan adjust the umbrellas beside and behind him. It seemed to him she'd been fiddling with the lighting a great deal longer than necessary.

"You said I could have anything I wanted for Christmas," she reminded him as she held the light meter up to his face. "I want this picture."

"It was a weak moment," he mumbled.

"Tough." Unsympathetic, Bryan stepped back to study the angles. There, the lighting was perfect, the shadows just where they should be. But... A long-suffering sigh came out. "Shade, stop glowering, will you?"

"I said you could take the picture. I didn't say it'd be pretty."

"No chance of that," she said under her breath.

Exasperated, she brushed at her hair and the thin gold band on her left hand caught the light. Shade watched it glimmer with the same sort of odd pleasure he always felt when it hit him that they were a team, in every way. With a grin, he joined his left hand with hers so that the twin rings they wore touched lightly.

"Sure you want this picture for Christmas? I'd thought of buying you ten pounds of French chocolate."

She narrowed her eyes, but her fingers laced with his. "A low blow, Colby. Dead low." Refusing to be distracted, she backed off. "I'll have my picture," she told him. "And if you want to be nasty, I'll buy my own chocolate. Some husbands," she continued as she walked back to the camera set on a tripod, "would cater to their wife's every whim when she's in my delicate condition."

He glanced down at the flat stomach under baggy overalls. It still dazed him that there was life growing there. Their life. When summer came again, they'd hold their first child. It wouldn't do to let her know he had to fight the urge to pamper her, to coddle her every moment. Instead, Shade shrugged and dipped his hands in his pockets.

"Not this one," he said lightly. "You knew what you were getting when you married me."

She looked at him through the viewfinder. His hands were in his pockets, but he wasn't relaxed. As always, his body was ready to move, his mind moving already. But in his eyes she saw the pleasure, the kindness and the love. Together they were making it work. He didn't smile, but Bryan did as she clicked the shutter.

"So I did," she murmured.

* * * * *

COMING NEXT MONTH!

If AFFAIRE ROYALE (Volume #35) makes you want to learn more about Princess Gabriella's royal family, you're in luck, because Nora Roberts's sweeping, sensuous saga continues next month!

In COMMAND PERFORMANCE (Volume #37), Prince Alexander, Gabriella's brother and the heir to the throne, becomes enchanted with Eve Hamilton, a resourceful American theatrical producer. But love must wait in the wings when the diabolical Deboque takes center stage—and threatens to bring down the curtain on the entire royal family!

The heart-stopping conclusion to this royal trilogy tells the tale of brother Bennett, THE PLAYBOY PRINCE (Volume #39). Lady Hannah Rothchild is far removed from Bennett's typical romantic interest. He's puzzled by his fascination for this quiet, well-bred Englishwoman— but what will he do when he discovers she's an espionage agent in disguise?

If fairy-tale dreams were ever to come true, they would take place in the sunny Mediterranean in a magical land like Cordina. Don't miss COMMAND PERFORMANCE and THE PLAYBOY PRINCE—and find out how two Prince Charmings finally meet their matches!

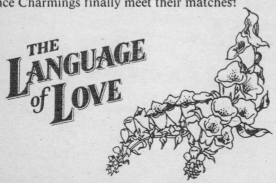

THE LANGUAGE of LOVE